FACING REALITY

A LOVE STORY

IAN BULL

Dear Ina,
Thank you for
reading my work!
Donald

Intersection Productions, Inc.

Studio City, California

Ian Bull/Intersection Productions, Inc.
Los Angeles, CA, 91604
www.IanBullAuthor.com

Publisher's Note: This is a work of fiction. Names, characters, places, and incidents are a product of the author's imagination. Locales and public names are sometimes used for atmospheric purposes. Any resemblance to actual people, living or dead, or to businesses, companies, events, institutions, or locales is completely coincidental.

Facing Reality/ Ian Bull. -- 1st ed.
ISBN 978-1-948873-15-4

Ian Bull is also the author of *Liars in Love,* set in San Francisco in 1980. He also writes *The Quintana Adventures,* a thriller series which includes *The Picture Kills,* and *Six Passengers, Five Parachutes.* The third book, *The Danger Game,* will be out in 2019. He also writes nonfiction under his full name, Donald Ian Bull.

You can find more writing and free downloads at:

Ianbullauthor.com

Or just email him and he'll send you a gift:

Ianbullauthor@gmail.com

Please write an honest review of this book! It's the best way for me to reach more readers. Just email me and I'll show you how.

To Los Angeles, my home. When I first arrived, I swore that it would only be for a few years, but people warned me that I'd stay for good. They were right, and I'm a better person for it.

The final story, the final chapter of western man, I believe, lies in Los Angeles.

—PHIL OCHS

This story takes place in the year 2000. Cell phones and emails are a part of life, but smart phones aren't here yet. Reality TV is exploding. TV Production is still shot on video tapes that you can hold in your hand. Not much else has changed.

CHAPTER 1

Paul wakes up to the sound of Maggie showering, and the first thought that enters his mind is how much money he owes. It's been this way for a month, ever since he moved into Maggie's apartment to hide from the bill collectors who keep calling and the car repo guys who keep chasing him for his Toyota Camry. He used to think of sex first thing in the morning, not bills. His eyes would open, and he'd catch a glimpse of Maggie's perfect tan skin crisscrossed with sheet marks. Then their eyes would meet, and they'd grab each other. This morning she slid out of bed while he was still asleep.

He kicks off the sheets and listens to her shower, humming and splashing, while the spring sun streams through the window. The sunshine drives back his worry and he sees himself frozen in this perfect moment – a morning in June in his 25th year, his life still ahead of him, and his best girlfriend of all time just ten feet away, naked and wet…but then his worry returns.

That, he realizes, was probably the highlight of his day, and he files it away in his brain for later. Paul does this often; he calls them his "movie moments" when he both experiences life and observes himself within it. Paul has plans to someday open his mental file cabinet and pull out all the movie moments he has ever had and recreate them as cinema, larger than life –

The door to the bathroom swings open and Maggie's head pops out. "Do you mind getting the paper before the sprinklers go on?" She closes the door without waiting for a response.

Paul jumps out of bed and pulls on jeans and a t-shirt, happy to have a task. After four years of college and a 3.8 GPA, he is more than qualified to fetch a paper. It might be his only job all day, but he'll do it and he'll do it well. He stumbles through the cool apartment and out into the sun.

Maggie lives in a Spanish style building with eight apartments facing a courtyard. The building starred in a film noir thriller from the 40s, shot in crisp black and white. In one great tracking shot, the rain-drenched hero walks from the street through the open archway into the courtyard, past a bubbling fountain and right up to the apartment of the femme fatale who would be his demise. Today the fountain is filled with dirt and the tall archway is blocked off with an iron gate. Paul holds it open and grabs a *Los Angeles Times* from the pile in front.

Maggie is pouring coffee when he gets back. Paul smooths the paper on the table for her and then sits down to watch her prepare her breakfast. Maggie's long brown hair is still wet after her shower, and Paul admires how her bathrobe perfectly frames her hourglass figure. Erotic thoughts flood him, but he keeps them to himself. He likes her like this in the morning – fresh, without makeup and intent on getting to work, oblivious to how that mere millimeter of terrycloth covering her ample bottom and small breasts can drive him nuts. He imagines walking up and spooning her from behind and breathing on her neck. She would act shocked, insisting that she looks terrible.

But he resists. She must get to work, and his love gestures are not welcome on a busy Monday morning. When they both had jobs, it was a different story. A little erotic affection used to bring them closer before they both rushed out the door to start their work weeks. But not anymore. She's doing him a huge favor letting him stay with her, so he must focus on being a helpful and productive boyfriend on the job hunt, and not a lazy and horny loser.

The phone rings. Maggie keeps pouring milk over her cereal.

"Aren't you going to get that?" Paul asks.

"It's a creditor looking for you. He called yesterday morning at the same time."

"Which one?"

She shrugs. "I don't know, I just hung up. I think they've figured out that you're living here, or hiding here, or whatever it is you're doing."

The answering machine takes the call, but the volume is down. Maggie moves next to the kitchen table, eating her Cheerios as she studies him. Paul can see that he's crossed some line in her mind. She looks settled and in control, and that control makes her look beautiful. Beautiful, because he is losing her.

"So, which is it?" she asks. "Are you living here? Or are you just hiding?"

"Both."

She shakes her head, disgusted by the answer. "Excuse me, I have a job to get to." She goes into the bedroom.

And what a job it is. Maggie is the personal assistant to an asshole who produces TV award shows. Every day she patiently organizes the man's entire life and then in a crowded production meeting he will throw his fruit salad at her because she hasn't taken out all the grapes. Their nickname for him is "The Screaming Asshole," a name he earns at least twice a week. It's a miserable way to make a living, but then again, she can pay the rent and Paul can't.

The sound of a sliding closet door brings him back – he's missing their show. Paul goes into the bedroom and props himself up against the headboard so he can watch Maggie dress. It's their ritual, regardless of their mood, like morning coffee.

She drops her robe and stands there in just her panties, staring at the clothes closet with legs apart, fists on her hips and her breasts out. She looks like a modern Vermeer, calculating every permutation of the professional woman's uniform. She finally breaks her gaze and grabs some pantyhose, holding them up like evidence of a crime.

"Ten hours a day, five days a week, I force half the skin on my body into these, so you can be a filmmaker."

"I'll wear them too if you want."

"You should. It'd be good research into what it's like to be a woman."

She pulls the nylon up each leg, imprisoning her flesh, then puts on a lacy bra that snaps in front. Then comes a black pencil skirt, a loose blue silk shirt with a big collar and a tight black jacket that flares at the wrists.

"That's it, movie's over."

"What about the makeup?" Paul complains.

"I'm out, I have to get some on the way," she mutters. "Then again, if Herr Director insists it be part of the show, he can always go buy me some."

Paul pulls out forty dollars from his jeans pocket. "Here, buy what you want."

Maggie looks at the money. "Is that all the cash you have?"

"No," he lies.

"What we need, forty dollars can't fix." Maggie walks out.

Ouch. Good one. He hears Maggie's keys tinkling. He must make his move. He jumps off the bed and darts into the living room before she can leave.

"How about I take you out tonight? We'll do Indian food and then go see Buster Keaton at the Silent Movie Theater."

Maggie pauses, blinking slowly, biting her lower lip.

"That's what normal people do, right?" Paul asks. "Come on, it'll be fun. I'll tell you all about the four job interviews I'm going to find today."

When she hears that line, her real smile comes back, flush with hope, and he can see that she still wants it to work.

"Okay," she nods. She kisses him on the lips and leaves for the day.

CHAPTER 2

Paul spends the morning on the phone, looking for work. He checks in with two temp agencies, then phones low-budget production companies about doing grip work on movie sets. Everyone asks for his resume, but no one is encouraging. He reads the paper, does the dishes, makes the bed, and cleans the bathroom. He has tomato soup with crackers for lunch. When the phone rings, he screens the callers. There are two creditors, one calling about his student loan, the other calling about a maxed-out Visa card. Two of Maggie's friends call and ask in worried voices whether Paul is *still* living there. There are no job offers.

At 2 p.m., he decides he must do some creative work to feed his soul. He can't work on his movie because he's broke, so he sits down at the computer and works on his new screenplay, since writing is free. It's a story about five genetically-engineered superkids who escape the lab facility where they were bred and go to New York to form an alternative rock band. The kids just want to play some kickass tunes while eluding the evil government agency that created them. But then in the underground music scene they butt heads with five powerful young aliens posing as a punk group, who are part of a scouting expedition to conquer Earth. The kids realize they must use their hidden super powers to save the planet, even though it means the government will trace them and it may ruin the group. The movie comes to an amazing climax in New York's legendary CBGBs in a literal "battle of the bands." Paul starts on page seven, writes for two hours and gets to page nine.

He emails resumes and checks in with a few job sites on the Internet. He gets no responses, and by 6 p.m. he figures the day is a wash, so he sits down to watch TV until Maggie gets home.

The phone rings. Paul mutes *The Jerry Springer Show* and leans forward to listen to the caller leave a message on the machine:

"Hello, this is Hans Mela at RTL German Television and we are looking for a cameraman tonight…"

Paul picks up the phone, mid message. "Hello, this is Paul Franti. You need a cameraman?"

"Yes, our regular shooter just canceled and there's a movie premiere we need to cover for our *Hollywood News Show*. Lars said you worked with us twice last year?" Hans asks.

"Yes," Paul answers. "I shot the David Hasselhoff record release party, and the lighting of the Christmas tree on the *Bold and the Beautiful*."

"Both good pieces. Can you meet our crew in an hour?"

CHAPTER 3

*F*lash *Flood* is on the marquee of the Mann's Chinese Theatre, in big red letters that scream "action thriller." Paul has noticed that when a film is bad, the studio hosts a big premiere, and from the small size of the crowd, Paul knows that *Flash Flood* must be a terrible summer movie. Any event at the Mann's Chinese is a cluster fuck for all the news crews covering it, even the small ones. Paul finds his reporter, Cindy, fighting to hold a spot in the camera line while straddling the camera and gear bag.

"Are you the RTL reporter?" Paul asks.

"Yes," she moans, "and the gear's getting trampled!"

Paul kneels and slides the Betacam camera from between her ankles. He unzips the gear bag, slaps a battery on the back, hooks up the audio transmitter, tests the microphone and hands it to Cindy.

"We're good to go," Paul says, and just in time. The first guests are already walking up the red carpet.

The studio publicist sticks them at the end of the TV camera line right next to the screaming paparazzi, where it will be hard to attract celebrities. But Cindy is a good entertainment journalist and she came prepared in a low-cut dress with a zippered front that pushes her boobs out, and soon there's a steady stream of young male TV stars agreeing to chat with her. The paparazzi scream at them, flooding everyone with a tsunami of flashbulbs. The other crews howl in protest, wanting the boys to talk to them, and the publicists are pissed that their news event has been hijacked by German television. Then the pushing starts.

Cindy interviews a hunk named Marco DiPippio who Paul frames in a tight chest shot. A screaming publicist yanks on his left arm, so

Paul pans left – and smacks his lens into the camera next to him. A dozen people push back, crushing him and Cindy against the metal barrier that pen in the paparazzi. Someone punches Paul in the back, and the $50,000 camera slips off his shoulder into empty air. In a microsecond, Paul turns, catches the camera on the way down, pulls it to his chest, spins in the air and lands on his back with the camera safe in his arms. He sees a flash of light as his skull bounces on the pavement.

When he wakes up, there's plenty of open pavement around him. The camera is cradled against his chest with the red tally light still on, which means the whole incident is captured on tape. His head hurts. Then he notices the circle of people staring down at him, and Cindy, scowling. A publicist breaks through the circle and kneels close to him.

"Do you have any kind of press credentials?"

Paul touches the back of his head. It's sticky. "I think I'm bleeding."

"If you don't have credentials, you both must leave now."

They leave without protest and make their way to the parking lot behind the theater. Cindy opens the tailgate of her sport utility vehicle and Paul slides the camera back into its case. His hair is wet, but the bump is still too huge for the blood to really start flowing. It just throbs. He ejects the one tape he shot.

"Just give me the hundred dollars, we'll call it a night."

"I don't have a hundred dollars. You're supposed to invoice them."

"You guys paged me to do this two hours ago. The only reason I agreed was because I'd be paid a hundred dollars in cash."

"No one told me that," she says.

"I just cracked my skull open to save your network from buying another camera."

"This never happens with our regular camera guy. And I don't even have enough footage to cut a story," she says.

"How much money do you have?"

Cindy laughs. "On me? Right now? Maybe fifty."

"I'll take it." Paul sticks out his hand.

Cindy smirks, laying the contempt on thick. She pulls out two twenties and a ten. Paul takes it and walks away. He knows they won't call him again. It's best to just get as much money as he can and safely get himself and his car back to Maggie's.

He walks down Hollywood Boulevard, feeling his skull throb with every step. He parked his Camry in the lot behind Musso and Frank's Grill, figuring it would be safer there than out on the street. But when he reaches the lot he spots a familiar brown Oldsmobile Cutlass with two men smoking inside. He can only see their shapes – one is small and skinny, the other one is large. He gets his key in the front door lock as the guys emerge.

"Paul Franti?"

Paul doesn't look up.

"If you're not going to pay for the car anymore, the owners would like it back."

Paul gets in and locks the door. The small guy comes up to the driver's side, while the big guy hangs back by the right rear tire, cop style. Great, Paul thinks. They've probably got guns too. Paul stares straight ahead as the small guy taps on the side glass with his pinkie ring.

"We're just doing our job, Mr. Franti, don't make us chase you."

"I'll call the dealership tomorrow." Paul starts the car.

The repo guy moves to block the car, but Paul pops the car into gear and zooms past him and out of the parking lot. But he goes into the street too fast, bottoms out, and smashes his head into the ceiling of his car, filling his brain with another white flash of pain. He makes it to the corner and turns left onto Hollywood Boulevard. He glances in the rearview mirror – the Oldsmobile Cutlass is behind him, but they miss the light.

His legs are shaking. The pain now flows through him and makes him so angry he punches the dashboard. Three years ago, he couldn't have imagined himself in this situation. He had a life, money in the bank, and he was fresh out of school with a future as a filmmaker. He had an award-winning short movie under his arm and he was ready to bend Los Angeles to his will. And here he is, almost a decade later, terrified, his sweat and blood staining the seat of a car he can no longer afford.

Paul turns onto Cahuenga into bad traffic. He glances in the rearview mirror. The Cutlass is back there somewhere, closing in. He feels like O.J. as their car inches forward in slow pursuit.

What kind of life is this? But what would he do instead? Give up and go to Law School? Get an MBA? He is thirty-one, it might be too late to change. This is why he hates Los Angeles traffic; it gives him way too much time to think.

Paul keeps turning down dark side streets. He needs a place to hide – he can't risk them following him back to Maggie's and knowing where she lives. He passes the ugly concrete buildings on Seward and spots The Darby Sound Company, with the gate open and the lights on, which means Big Andy is still in there mixing. He turns in and parks.

Perfect, he thinks. He'll just sink into a deep plush sofa in a darkened audio booth and let Andy's latest hip hop mix lull him to sleep.

Paul rings the doorbell and steps back so Andy can see him from the upstairs window. Andy waves just as Paul sees the Cutlass drive by. He hears the brakes screech. The car is coming back.

"Andy! Shut the gate!"

Andy shrugs through the window and points at his ear. He can't hear him.

"Shut the gate so I can keep my car!"

Andy hits a button and the gate inches forward. Paul runs and pushes the gate in its track to help it along. The Cutlass roars back, slams into drive and tries to drive inside but the gate locks in time.

The repo guys get out and Paul sees their faces for the first time. They are around his age and already embrace their roles in life – the beefy guy with the goatee wearing the motorcycle jacket is the Enforcer, and the small guy in the black suit is the Businessman.

The Businessman holds up his hands. "Is it worth it to exhaust yourself like this? We're going to get the car anyway."

"Sorry. I've got to keep this car. I'm dead without it."

"Next time, don't make us chase you. It gets everybody's adrenaline pumping, and that's how someone gets hurt."

The repo men get in their car and drive away. Paul hears crickets and smells night blooming jasmine. That was a movie moment, Paul thinks, and he files it away. And they were very polite, considering what he's put them through.

Upstairs, Andy greets him with a hug and Paul feels all 260 Midwestern pounds of him, with his cornhusker hair and his baggy hip hop outfit. Andy, his best friend from college, and his only friend left from that brief time when they thought all things were possible.

"Are you doing speed? You're way too skinny."

Paul frowns. "No, I'm not doing speed. I'm just anxious and starving to death. And tonight, I got this bump." Paul tilts his wounded head for Andy to see. Andy winces.

"How big is it?" Paul asks.

"It's a walnut. But it's stopped bleeding, so quit touching it."

"I need to lie down."

"You can't sleep. You might go into a coma or something."

Andy puts him in an office chair, opens the first aid kit and rips open a roll of gauze which he wraps around Paul's sticky head.

"Things change, huh Andy?"

"Yup. Things change."

They'd driven out from Andover College together. Paul had an agent then and started going to meetings, all because he did a short film everybody loved. Andy had wanted to make films too, but found mixing and audio work easier, which Paul had looked down on as settling for less.

But while Paul had slaved on his art in the eight years since, Andy had worked nine-to-five, and met all kinds of people. Now Andy is mixing sound for commercials during the day and producing music demos for bands at night. He even owns a field audio rig for news shoots and documentaries. He is on a creative path and has money in his wallet while Paul is two steps above a street person.

"How late are you mixing tonight?"

"Until dawn. The band's due any minute. When you rang the bell, I thought you were them – they're called XXX-Tra, four brothers from UCLA spending their parents' money, pretending to be 'gangstas.' One even went to the Berklee College of Music."

"Can I stay?"

"Sure, you'll be my assistant. Work off some of that debt you owe me."

Andy pats the bandage. It's not holding, so he tapes down another layer of gauze. A white helmet slowly takes shape.

"Funny you stopped by. A producer called today, some guy named Joel. He's looking for somebody to do audio on a network special. He's renting my rig. If you want, I can pass your name on to him."

"Audio?" Paul asks. "If anything, I'm a shooter. I don't know audio."

"Fine. Turn it down."

Paul reconsiders the offer. "A network special, huh?"

"Yup, except there's never anything special about a network special. And it's a 'reality show,' so you know it's a shit load of work, chasing people through the streets with a camera and a boom pole."

"But it's a job."

"Exactly. And if you want a job, I'll recommend you."

The bandages are still loose. Andy takes off his knit cap and pulls it down over Paul's head, holding in the entire white and red mess. The buzzer rings.

"XXX-Tra is in the house. Let's get to work."

CHAPTER 4

There's no sign of any repo men at six-thirty in the morning, so Paul feels safe enough to drive his fugitive Camry back to Maggie's apartment. He putters down Highland Boulevard against the morning traffic heading into Hollywood. At the stoplight, he glances over and sees men sipping coffee alongside women putting on lipstick in the rearview mirrors, already on their way to their studio jobs, Paul thinks. Meanwhile, he's on his way home with fifty bucks to his name.

He gets to Cochran Avenue, circles the block to check for the repo men again, then turns into the driveway and coasts between the buildings into a one-car wooden garage behind Maggie's building. Hers is the only unit that comes with a garage, and she lets him use it to hide his car.

Paul waits and lets the cool dark of the garage soothe him. It's not even seven yet and it's already eighty degrees outside. His head throbs. He touches the back of Andy's knit cap where his wound is. It's still tender, even with all the gauze bandages Andy stuck under there.

Paul takes a breath. Maggie isn't going to be happy. Time to go inside.

When he gets to her front door he finds Rupert, the pompous English actor who lives upstairs, handing her the morning paper. That's *his* job.

"Paul. You look ravished," Rupert grins.

"Rupert. You look English." Paul grins back and steps inside.

Paul collapses on the couch while Rupert and Maggie chat about his big audition that afternoon. She wishes Rupert good luck, shuts the door, and all her cheeriness disappears. "I waited for you at the theater last night for an hour."

"I got a job shooting video last night. I left you a note."

"And I left a message on the machine telling you I'd meet you at the theater. You should have called me at work."

"I'm sorry, I was in a rush. I thought you'd come home."

"What kind of job keeps you out all night? Were you shooting porn again?"

"No, and I only shot porn <u>once</u>. This was a movie premiere, and some repo men found me there. I stayed at Andy's all night, working for him, just like I said in the other message I left you, the second time I called. You must have been home by then."

"I was. I just wasn't picking up," she replies.

Paul considers ripping off his knit cap and showing off his wound, but going for pity seems the wrong move right now. She might not even care at all, which would make it hurt even worse.

"Something else happened last night," he says. "I may be up for a real job, it's a network special, doing audio. Andy referred me."

Maggie crosses her arms, furrows her brow, and examines him.

"Everything's taking longer than I planned," Paul pleads. "But I'll make it. I promise. I have to make it."

Maggie sighs with a mix of pity and regret. "I used to feel that way."

Paul remembers – before they'd met, Maggie struggled to make it as an art director for films until starvation made her take a desk job.

Maggie grabs her coffee cup and heads for the bedroom. Paul gets off the couch to follow her, but Maggie puts her hand up.

"No way. I'm not giving you any show today," she says.

Paul lays his head back against the couch cushion and feels his wound throb straight through his body all the way down to his feet. The phone rings. Paul imagines the creditor on the other end, intent on harassing him. The machine finally picks up, and Paul closes his eyes and falls asleep.

When he wakes up, Maggie is gone.

Paul staggers to the shower. He takes off all his clothes except for the knit cap, then stands in front of the mirror and gently rolls it off his head. Gauze, hair, and blood have hardened into a red and white helmet. He tries lifting it off, but clotted blood keeps it glued in place.

Usually he considers himself passably handsome, but this morning he looks ridiculous. He is too skinny – he can see the ribs on his chest and too many bones on his face, like gaunt angles on pasty white skin. His lips are white, his teeth grey, his brown hair is greasy, and it's all topped off with a dorky red and white helmet. He looks like a vampire geek.

And his head still throbs, shooting pain straight down to his heels on the tile floor. He shivers. Time to get his withered nuts into a shower before he freezes those off, too. He tests the hot water over his hands then eases his shoulders under the stream. The hot steam loosens everything, and his bandage helmet falls off except for one strip of gauze that's still stuck to his head, and it swings like a pendulum for a moment before the weight of the wet paper tugs the scab clean off. Paul touches the gash. Should he risk it? He eases his head under the warm water. It stings, then feels wonderful.

He steps out of the shower, wipes the steam off the mirror, then twists himself into a pretzel trying to find his wound both in the reflection of Maggie's hand mirror and in the bathroom cabinet mirror, but the cut is too high on his head to see. Instead, he wraps his head with a turban of toilet paper, puts on a baseball cap, and takes two aspirin.

It comes down to luck, Paul thinks. All I need is to get lucky. Meet people. Quit being so independent. Collaborate. It's who you know, just like an old boys' club.

I'm making a movie alone in a town full of people who work together all the time, and I can't do it by myself anymore.

He checks his pupils in the mirror and both are the same size. If he were in serious trouble he'd know by now. But he needs help getting to sleep. He thinks about masturbating, but too much of his body is throbbing already. He settles for a slug of wine out of the open bottle in the refrigerator, unplugs the phone, closes the blinds, climbs into bed and passes out.

He dreams he is thirteen and back in the living room of his mom's house in Andover, Massachusetts, with his mom, sister, and all the neighborhood kids. Everyone is there to see Paul's feature film, *Liars Dice*, the one he's been working on for three years on a shoestring budget.

But there's no VCR, only his grandfather's 8mm film projector from the garage, and his film is Super 16mm, not 8mm – and it'll never fit on the projector. He opens the can and looks at his film – and magically it shrinks from 16mm down to 8mm, on a tiny inadequate spool. After all that work, the film is now nowhere near ninety minutes, which is the minimum for feature length. It shrank magically down to ten minutes, tops.

The kids are getting restless, especially the mean ones in the back who never liked him – like Sam Ricci and Frank Jefferson. Kids in the front row are talking about how much they liked the action thriller, *Flash Flood,* and how this film better be as good.

Paul threads his film and hits the *Run Forward* button. His movie appears on a sheet stretched across the fake fireplace. It's a clever romantic comedy about two thieves who fall in love, except he's acting out all the parts by himself in bad costumes in his Mom's backyard. Paul is too scared to look back at the audience, but he feels their anger. Somebody hits him in the neck with spit wad. He hears a hum – the projector is vibrating. He can't touch it because it's now red hot and it's shaking towards him, about to fall off the table –

– it's his pager, vibrating on the bed stand. He bolts awake and the sheet comes up with him, glued to his head by a patch of dried blood. Paul pulls the sheet off slowly. There's a blood stain, and his tissue turban and baseball cap are lost in the sheets somewhere. The pager shows a number with a 310 area code. He plugs the phone back in the wall and dials. A male receptionist answers.

"ABS Producer's Lab, Mr. Joel Cuvney's office."

"This is Paul Franti, I'm returning a page?"

"Please hold."

Paul listens to a loop of TV commercial music. I'm on hold and bleeding to death, Paul thinks.

He looks at the bed – the blood stain is bad. Maggie will be pissed. She is upgrading her apartment and the bedroom is all she could afford to make nice so far. She'd dropped a dime on a sleigh bed with oak side tables and Italian linen, a framed French Art Nouveau Poster, velvet throw pillows and little packets of potpourri next to scented candles, and Paul dumped his blood right in the middle of it.

Someone comes on. "Paul! It's Joel Cuvney. I got your name from Big Andy."

"Sure! He told me you might call."

"Can you come in today to talk?"

"When were you thinking?"

"How about now? My office is in Century City, in the Towers."

"Hang on, let me check." Paul holds his hand over the phone for a few seconds, then comes back.

"I have one meeting this morning, but I think I can get out of it."

"Great. Scott will come back on the line and give you the info."

Paul hears the click and is back on hold.

CHAPTER 5

T he reception area is done up like Whoville from the Dr. Suess book, with twisting furniture and paisley walls. Paul is nervous, but prepared. He wears chino pants and a clean dress shirt, with a new baseball cap on his rebandaged head. He even shaved twice to eliminate any hint of beard – the younger he looks, the better.

Before driving over, he downloaded some trade articles about Joel Cuvney and the ABS Producers Lab. It's a satellite company the Fox network established to give "total creative freedom" to young producers "destined to reinvent the medium of television." That scares Paul. "Total creative freedom" means the company has been given no real money. That's the trade-off; the network gives them nothing substantial to risk, but they have total freedom to waste it however they like. He hoped the job would pull down at least a union wage, but now he knows they'll pay him far less per hour than what they paid the designer to do the lobby.

What intrigues him the most, however, is a line from a *Hollywood Reporter* article that said Joel Cuvney is teaming up with Dwight Werner on a "network special."

Dwight Werner is a documentary filmmaker loved by critics, his films are shown in film classes around the country, but he has never been a commercial success except maybe back in the 1980s. People consider his work either hard-to-understand masterpieces, or the Emperor's New Clothes. So why is he doing a network special?

Paul remembers only one of his films, *Daytona,* a plodding three-hour exposé of college Spring Break at Daytona Beach, Florida. He remembers it because he had just been to Daytona on Spring Break himself and had gotten drunk on mescal, stoned on pot, high on ecstasy, laid by a redhead from Michigan State, robbed by Townies, survived on waffles and Spudnuts, was beaten up by roadies from MTV, then got laid again by a brunette handing out free cigarettes on the beach, all in seventy-two hours, and he had only foggy memories of any of it. He'd gone to the movie *Daytona* hoping it would trigger some memories, but Dwight Werner's film was about the local Daytona soda delivery boy and how hard he worked while all the college kids were partying, which was so boring Paul fell asleep. He found out later that the documentary had won awards at several film festivals and he contemplated renting it to see if he'd missed the point.

Paul sinks back in the lobby sofa and stares up at the bowling pin clock mounted on the ceiling. He'd been there thirty minutes already. Were they blowing him off? A door shaped like a cello opens and a male model in black slacks and an ironed Gold's Gym t-shirt strides across the carpet and shakes his hand.

"Paul? Scott. Please, come this way. Joel and Dwight are in a meeting with the head of production, they'll be right in."

Paul steps through the cello door into a regular office. As Paul trails Scott through the maze of Dilbert cubicles, he shakes off the creeping fear that he too is destined for a cubicle like the rest of humanity. He is glad to get to Joel's room where he can sit on another couch and stare out the window.

"Would you like some coffee? Tea?"

"Just water."

"Easy enough," and Scott opens a small refrigerator by the desk and hands him an Evian bottle. Scott disappears. Paul sips.

How many of these offices has Paul been in? For script pitches, maybe ... fifty? Then he lost his agent. For production jobs, maybe another ... forty? Lunches were far fewer. The suits considered him worthy of that tax deduction for only about three months, when his short film was still hot.

Joel Cuvney and Dwight Werner suddenly are in the room. Paul shifts to get off the couch, but they all brush palms and sit down before Paul can even move. Joel slides behind his desk and Dwight plops down in the easy chair across from Paul.

"Paul, thanks for coming in. I see you took one of my waters," Joel says.

Paul sits frozen, feeling like he has egg on his face, while Joel paws through his stack of pink messages from the receptionist. I should've asked for coffee, Paul thinks.

Paul looks at Dwight. He is a squat man in his 50s, built like a fireplug, with sandy grey hair in a Caesar haircut. His whole body is rigid except for his right leg, which shakes like a piston on the ball of his foot. The rest of him is frozen, staring. This man is a famous filmmaker, but he looks like an angrier version of Paul's own dad.

Joel rocks back and forth in his executive chair. Joel is younger than Paul by maybe two years, with a plain long face and thinning black hair, but he has the confident casualness of someone born to a high station in life. Paul figures his family is well off, because he is far too young to have moved up from the mailroom. This job was bestowed upon him. Joel has his own nervous tic as well – an Omega watch he keeps twisting on his wrist, unhooking and hooking the metal clasp.

It's hard to figure out their relationship. Does the famous Dwight Werner truly answer to the younger Joel? Or is Joel the tiny obligatory leash the network put on Dwight, who intends to do what he wants anyway, as long as he comes in on budget?

Joel opens first. "Paul. Tell us about yourself."

"I've done audio with Big Andy for years. I can work a mixer and hold up a boom for ten hours straight without a break." Paul claps his hands, full of energy.

"If Andy referred you, I'm sure you're qualified. What we want is for you to tell us about you. Your hopes and dreams," Joel says with a straight face.

Damn, Paul thinks, it was a trick question. He decides on the short version.

"I'm from Andover, Massachusetts. I grew up watching a lot of TV, and then as a teenager I'd go to the movies three or four times a week. I still do."

The two men stare.

Documentaries, Paul thinks, I must mention documentaries.

"I'd see comedies, dramas, foreign films, and documentaries."

Dwight perks up. "You like reality?"

"I love reality."

"What do you like?"

Paul should remember something, quick. His memory bank kicks out a list:

"I like *Harlan County, USA ... Roger and Me ... My Brother's Keeper ... Paisan ... Titticut Follies ... Daytona...*"

"You liked *Daytona?*" Dwight asks.

"It was wonderful. It was a side of spring break no one ever sees."

Dwight stares at Paul. What *does* that stare mean?

"How'd you end up on the West Coast?" Joel asks.

"In college, I did a short film. It's called *Breakneck Speed*, and it won a lot of festivals in the short film category."

"Which ones?" Dwight asks.

"Chicago, Black Maria, Mill Valley…"

"You won the best short film at the Chicago Film Festival?" Joel's eyes narrow.

"Yup. And then I came out to Los Angeles and I've been here ever since."

"Have you written anything?"

"Seven screenplays. I optioned two, and sold one erotic thriller that never got made. So, I decided I'd just make my own feature, like I did with my short film."

"Don't tell me," Joel teases, "you're doing *Breakneck Speed 2.*"

"I wish," Paul laughs, "because maybe it'd be done by now. It's called *Liars Dice,* and it's about a man and woman who work as thieves, and they meet and fall in love, only they can't trust one another. I shot a third of it and then ran out of money, so I cut a trailer and now I'm showing it around town trying to raise the money to finish it."

"You're one of those guys you read about who makes a movie with credit cards and gets catapulted to fame and fortune."

"Except right now, my credit cards are all maxed out."

Dwight's leg stops shaking and Joel stops playing with watch. Paul can't decide if that's a bad sign or a good sign.

"What about audio?" Dwight asks.

Paul feels the flop sweat pouring down the back of his neck and into his shirt. *I should have talked about audio.* Your hopes and dreams must fit the job they're offering.

"I shoot too, but I prefer doing sound. It carries so much of the story. I go into each job thinking that the sound is just as crucial as picture," Paul says.

"Do you own your own rig?" Dwight asks. A good question; ownership indicates how serious one is about their craft. Paul decides to lie.

"I co-own one with a friend. Joel knows him – Big Andy. Our kit has a Shure mixer, three Sennheiser microphones, three lavs, and four Lectrosonic wireless microphones. Between the two of us the rig is always out working. We do junkets, industrials, but mostly entertainment news. And docs. Lots of docs."

Joel and Dwight nod. Maybe they like what they're hearing.

A tingle of regret goes up Paul's spine. Where did that lie come from? He prays for the questions to stop.

Joel and Dwight lean back and look at each other and trade a secret message. Joel speaks first. "Paul, you're fantastic. You're a filmmaker in your own right, and you own a business. You're a one-man operation, which is how you have to be today."

He's buttering me up, Paul thinks. Now he's going to bend me over.

Joel leans forward in his chair plops his hands on his desk. "But we're really looking for someone younger who's just starting out. This project is a lot of work with many hours in the field, and it sounds like you've already gone through that stage in your career."

"I thought this was a network special," Paul says.

"It is. But it's a new documentary-reality hybrid, and we're inventing it as we speak. And, like a lot of hybrids, it's fragile, and we don't have the time, money, or resources a regular network special commands."

Paul oversold himself; he is *too* qualified, and he doesn't even know audio. He considers brown nosing Dwight about what a privilege it would be to work with such a famous filmmaker, but he knows the drill – be gracious, get out, and cry in the car.

"I completely understand," Paul says. And if you guys have any trouble finding someone, just call me and I'll pass on some names."

Paul stands up for the first time since they walked in the room, shakes their hands and gives them as smile and a wave as he walks out the door.

He stops after six steps. Parking. He must get validated or he'll be stuck with a ten-dollar parking bill he can't afford. He turns on his heel and walks back into Joel's office with the parking stub in his hand. Both Dwight and Joel stare at him open-mouthed, as if he's naked and painted blue.

"I'm sorry to interrupt. Do you give stickers for parking?"

"The back of your shirt," Joel whispers. "It's covered in blood."

Paul stretches to see over his shoulder. The back of his white dress shirt is stained red down past his shoulder blades. Then he sees the red stain on the couch where he'd just been sitting. That wasn't flop sweat dripping down his neck, it was blood. He sits back down and slowly pulls off his hat, and the new bandages fall off with it. Paul lets everything drop to the floor. He doesn't care anymore.

Dwight peers down at his scalp. "You need stitches. Why didn't you go see a doctor?"

"I'm broke. That's the damn fucking truth."

Joel peeks too. "Yuck. How did you do that?"

"I was shooting video at a movie premiere and someone punched me. I had to dive to the pavement to save the camera."

"Did you save it?" asks Dwight.

"Yup. And I only made fifty bucks."

Dwight smiles. "Joel, I think we found our guy."

CHAPTER 6

P aul lies face down on an examining table while the nurse shaves his scalp around the wound. She stops to dab his oozing skull with fresh gauze then tosses it in a metal bowl already half full of red cotton. "You should have treated this earlier," she scolds. "The wound will be much harder to sew up now."

It turns out that two doctors have offices on the same floor as the ABS Producers Lab: one is a plastic surgeon named Dr. Chapman and the other is Dr. Rosenfeld, a urologist who specializes in penis enlargements. Joel knows them both. The urologist had ten patients waiting, but the plastic surgeon was done for the day and agreed to do a quick stitch job on Paul for no charge, once Joel asked. Joel must know him well.

The nurse snips more hair then goes back to shaving. "You're going to have a shaved patch for a while. It'll grow in funny."

"How many stitches?"

"Three, maybe four. That's the trouble with scalp wounds, they're not that serious but they just keep bleeding. There, I'm done. The doctor will be right in."

The nurse leaves, the sound of her feet fading away. The room is quiet even with the door open. Life is pleasant on the 34th floor. He turns his head and sees a phone on the wall, a foot away from him. He reaches up, dials 9 and then Maggie's number and waits for the machine to beep.

"Hey, it's me. I'm getting sewn up now and I'll be home soon. I can explain everything, and if anything is ruined, I'll replace it."

He hangs up, glad that he called. She will walk in any minute and find the bloody sheets floating in water in the kitchen sink and want to kill him.

Dr. Chapman, Joel, and Dwight walk in, all laughing about some private joke. Paul never even sees the doctor, he just grabs Paul's head and turns him face down.

"The anesthetic will hurt at first, then go numb. You'll feel it twice."

He holds Paul down by the neck and pokes the needle right into the cut, which stings worse than when he fell in the first place. But then the pain fades away for the first time in eighteen hours.

"How are you feeling?" Joel asks.

"Mostly embarrassed. Thank you." From the silence, Paul assumes they are all trading glances. He is vaguely aware of the doctor lacing up his skin like a football.

"Paul, we should talk about the project," Joel says. "We need someone right away."

Paul hears a watch clasp clicking and a rubber sole squeaking on linoleum. Both men's tics are back. "I'm listening. I'm a captive audience."

"Jedidiah Kincaid himself, the president of the network, picked six producers to run the ABS Producers Lab and told us to 'change television.' I am one of those producers. I've always deeply respected Dwight's work and I wanted to be the one to pull him out of obscurity and groom him for a huge commercial audience. So, I called him up. And the idea we developed together is nothing short of stunning. Right Dwight?"

Dwight clears his throat. Paul can tell that he didn't like Joel's little speech.

"My work is based on a simple idea – if you watch someone long enough, something interesting will happen," Dwight says, "and if you have enough interesting moments, you have a film. Or in this case, a television network special, shot on video –"

Joel interrupts. "What blows me away about Dwight's work is that he finds a subculture: kids on spring break, old folks in a retirement home, losers at the race track, people about whom we have preconceived notions. Then he shows the audience that they're people just like us, and he blasts all those notions right out of the water. I knew that simple idea would work for network television, if we find the *right* subculture –"

Dwight interrupts him right back. "I picked homeless youth."

"Homeless youth?" Paul asks.

The doctor finishes his stitching. "Done."

"Hank, thank you so much, especially on such short notice," Joel says.

"Hey, I love just listening to you guys. What you do is nuts. Use the room as long as you like." The doctor chuckles and leaves before Paul can thank him. Paul sits up. Joel and Dwight sit in identical chairs six feet apart from one another, staring right at him. Paul touches the stitches and feels them sticking up like barbed wire.

Dwight keeps talking. "We found a tribe of homeless kids past downtown on the other side of the L.A. River, living in an abandoned brewery. We've been following them twenty-four hours a day for six weeks now."

"How old are they?" Paul asks.

"All over eighteen," interrupts Joel, "so they can all sign their own permission releases. We had to go through a lot of back alleys and weed through some dull losers to find the right four kids. Poverty makes most people boring. But the ones we found are great. Completely watchable. On tape, they pop right out at you."

Dwight explodes. "This culture abandons its youth! It ignores the disenfranchised and criminalizes those forced to live on the fringe!" Dwight shouts at Paul. "Poverty is relentless, grinding away at the spirit, crushing people, all of whom, if given the chance, could be brilliant and alive! It's reprehensible. I want all the couch potatoes in this fucking country to see that!"

Joel shakes his head and laughs. "Sure, but is it entertaining?"

Paul feels odd; these men are arguing with one another while looking at him, but he has nothing to say. Dwight stares at him and sends over his next volley to Joel.

"My goal isn't to entertain. My goal is to confront. To create something that when you see it, you can't look away. That's entertainment, too."

Dwight stares at Paul with steel eyes. His leg is a vibrating blur.

"But we've got a late prime time slot, so we need a little sex and violence to spice up the 'grinding poverty,'" Joel explains to Paul. "The kids have been doing some boffing, but not enough. But I have my hopes." Joel twists his wristwatch at lightning speed.

"They're surviving! They're not interested in boffing!" Dwight shouts at Paul.

"Everybody's interesting in boffing!" Joel shouts at Paul.

Paul is the tip of a very fragile triangle. He touches his new scar.

"What do you need from me?"

"We need someone who can do audio in the field with our cameraman," Joel says.

"If we're following these kids, how do you direct?" Paul asks.

"I rigged a microwave transmitter to the camera that sends a video signal to monitors in a truck parked outside, or to a small portable TV monitor that I carry. The cameraman wears a headset so I can direct his shots via walkie-talkie, but you'll never hear me," says Dwight. "You'll be too busy getting the audio with your boom and the radio microphones that we strap to the kids. You just take visual cues from the cameraman."

Joel leans forward. "Enough technical chit chat. Do you want to do it?"

"How many hours a day of shooting is it?"

"This was an issue for our last audio guy." Joel warns. "We need someone who's willing to work."

"What does that mean? Twelve hours a day?" Paul aims high.

Both Dwight and Joel shift but neither say anything.

"Time and a half after twelve hours? Is that it? That's standard on low budget features."

Dwight shakes his head. The edge of his mouth turns down in disappointment.

"What? What did I say?"

"It's not you. It's just that my work is my passion, so I never end up thinking about it in terms of hours I must work."

"I'm just asking what the hours are, how many weeks the job lasts, and how much you pay. That's not a weird thing to ask when you're taking a job," Paul explains.

Paul stands his ground. Joel sighs. The logic of this request finally breaks him.

"The job is for another six weeks. We pay a thousand dollars a week. But the hours change. You could work five hours a day, or twelve. Or eighteen. Even twenty. And we shoot six days a week."

Paul ponders these two men, crammed together with him in a doctor's tiny examining room, one madly twisting his wristwatch, the other with a trembling leg, their blank faces barely concealing how much they hate one another. It's another movie moment, a surreal one that he files away in his mental filing cabinet under "bizarre."

He has no choice; he must take the job. Paul wonders if he can spend six weeks with them – or anybody – 24 hours a day, working in spaces smaller than this one. He just hopes Dwight and his cameraman eat healthy diets, because soon enough he'll be with them so often he'll be able to ID them from their body odor and the smell of their farts.

"It sounds like a lot of work for the money."

"True, but you won't have time to spend a lot either," Joel says. "Plus, we'll rent your audio rig from you, so you'll make some more money that way."

You mean Andy will make more money, Paul thinks. Andy has the best deal; he'll be making money in his sleep while Paul works. Paul does some quick calculating. He'd make enough to pay off some credit card debt, some of the car, and pay Maggie for back rent and groceries maybe…

"It sounds like a great project. I'd love it if you'd hire me," Paul says, and all the men smile with relief and they all shake hands.

But Paul has questions – like what happened to the other audio guy? It's never a good sign when you're replacing someone on a troubled project. Are they hiring him out of desperation? And is there a decent bathroom in this abandoned brewery across the river? And who are these homeless kids?

"We'll pull you some tapes and send them over later," Dwight says.

"Scott has your paperwork in the office," Joel says. "When do I start?"

"Tomorrow night." Dwight says.

CHAPTER 7

P aul, wearing just shorts, sits in a kitchen chair with a sheet around him while Maggie uses the electric razor to shave his hair down to stubble to match the shaved patch on the top of his head. She is having fun, which makes it fun for Paul. The pizza and beer help too, along with the fact that he has a job.

The phone call made all the difference, Paul thinks. He came home expecting to be crucified, but the bloody sheets scared her. Then she tortured herself over the message that he left; she guessed that he must have been hurt in the morning and didn't tell her and regretted not being nice. And then he came home with good news about work, and things got all lovey-dovey.

He let his mind drift to the job. His invaluable input would save this show, then he'd be recognized for his genius and attract the attention of the network honchos, then they'd offer him directing jobs, he'd get in the union, and he would finish his film. The film would get great reviews, his movie would be a hit and he'd get a three-picture deal.

The razor clicks off. Maggie pauses to assess her work.

"It's still a little uneven. I should really just shave you bald."

"Bald will happen soon enough, we don't need to be rushing things."

Maggie touches his head, enjoying the bristles. "I'll bring out the shaving cream, a razor, and lots of towels and warm water. It'll be sexy."

"Only if I can shave you first."

Maggie giggles. He grabs her baggy boxers and pulls her to him. She grabs both sides of his fuzzy head and inhales her desire through her teeth. He pulls her down for a kiss and she more than meets him halfway.

"I like how you look with short hair," she says when she comes up for air.

"Really? And how's that?"

"Like a bad boy. Especially with that scar on your head."

Paul drops the sheet and spots his reflection in the dark kitchen window. It takes a moment for him to adjust. He looks better, like he went through something and came out stronger on the other side.

"I look like a war veteran." He finishes the last inch of another Corona and grabs the broom to sweep up his hair.

"Leave that."

"You're just going to wake up to a mess in the morning and be pissed."

She grabs the broom from him. "Oh yeah? You think so, Zipperhead?"

His opens his eyes wide in mock insult. She backs away in mock fear. He growls. That's the signal. She turns and runs, but he catches up to her at the bedroom door. He grabs the elastic of her boxers and yanks the cotton down over one butt cheek just as she dives for the bed. She lands face down, with her bottom in the air, laughing hysterically into a pillow. He launches himself on top of her and gives her big beautiful ass a healthy slap.

Then she executes a surprise scissors kick, catches him in a vise grip and twists. She's suddenly straddling him. The giggling stops. Together they yank his shorts off and don't even bother with her boxers. She just yanks them to one side, grabs him and slides him inside her. They both sigh. They're home again, after a very long time.

The next morning the phone wakes them up. Maggie answers.

"Hello? Now? It's 7:30 in the morning ... okay, he'll be right out to get it." Maggie hangs up. "There's a runner from the network out in front of the building with a delivery for you."

Paul stares at the phone, resenting it. He pulls on some jeans and a baggy sweatshirt to cover his morning erection. A surfer dude with a cell phone strapped to his waist stands on the other side of the iron gate. Paul pushes open the door and signs for the tapes as the guy grins behind his Oakley sunglasses.

"Tell the lady I apologize for the interruption," he snickers.

Paul ignores him and goes back inside. Maggie is already up; she swept the kitchen floor and brewed coffee, which means there is little chance he can lure her back to bed. He rips open the box and inside are four VHS tapes labeled CASTING – ABS Movie of the Week Project. Each tape had a different name – Trent, Jodi, Ilima and Duncan.

"What is it?" Maggie asks, handing him a coffee mug.

"It must be the four kids from the show."

"Were they cast? I thought they were real."

"I guess they're both. They're real but there was a casting process."

"Great. This'll be better than Saturday morning cartoons," Maggie says. She grabs the tape labeled Trent and sticks it in the VCR, plops down on the futon couch and zaps the remote. Paul slides down next to her.

Trent comes on screen: African-American, light-skinned with dark black eyes, thin and wispy, with brown hair in dreadlocks. He's sits in a chair and leans against a cement wall, just balancing on the chair's back legs. A glaring light source glares down from above – probably a bare light bulb just off screen. Trent looks smart, jaded, bored and awkward all at the same time. He lights a cigarette and inhales deeply.

Dwight's voice asks a question. "Will you tell me the story?"

"Which one?"

"The one about traveling across the country from New York."

"The whole thing?"

"Whatever part you want."

Trent flicks the ash off his cigarette. "I'm originally from Crown Heights, in Brooklyn, but I haven't been home for a long time. For a year, I was living on the streets and crashing on my friends' sofas, because whenever I would go home my Dad and I would kick the shit out of each other. I sliced his face open with my ring and he broke my middle finger."

Trent flips the camera the bird with his left hand, and his middle finger is bent thirty-degrees halfway up.

"Do you plan to get that fixed?" Dwight asks off screen.

"No way. Some girls love it, if you know what I mean."

"So how did you end up here?"

"My Dad is a big music collector and he had tons of old records and CDs. We lived like cockroaches, but hey, he always took care of the collection. When they were out, I went in there and took that shit, and I left a note telling him I did. And I didn't take nothing from my mom or my sister."

"And what did you do with it?"

"I got three thousand dollars in thirty minutes and I bought a bus ticket and left town. He's probably still running the streets of Brooklyn looking for me, and I'm clear across the country."

"So how was your trip across our great nation?"

Trent smiles, and holds up his finger and recites a poem:

> *"I'm a traveling black man, learning what I can,*
> *my life an education, in containing frustration...*
> *This country don't see me, but I see you. All of you."*

Trent drops his finger, his poem done.

"You talk in rhyme a lot?"

"When it hits me." Trent flicks his cigarette away.

Dwight adjusts the camera. "You say your trip was 'an education in frustration.' Can you give me an example?"

"Traveling cross-country by bus you stop a lot. The bus driver will wait for a half an hour for some stupid white woman who's keeping everyone waiting, and she won't even thank him. But if I keep the guy waiting thirty seconds, he thinks I'm fucking with his schedule and he'll leave without me. I'm not asking for permission to be late, that's not what I'm saying. I'm saying that when you're black you grow up knowing you must be back on the bus *first,* otherwise the bus goes. White people don't worry about that when they're sitting on the toilet in a bus station trying to do their business. It never even enters their minds. That's the stuff that gets to you after a while.

This one time I'm in the bus station in butt fuck Ohio, starving, trying to buy soda and chips and just get back on the bus, but the guy behind the counter won't take my money. He just ignores me and rings up all the other people in line behind me. And I couldn't put the chips back because I'd already opened the bag, and if I just left I'd be shoplifting, which I think is what the guy *really* wanted me to do. I put ten bucks on the counter and left, but by the time I got back to the gate the bus was already gone."

"So, you're convinced all that was racially motivated?"

On tape, Trent looks incredulous. "Are you even listening to me, dude?"

"It was just a question."

"After that I was *not* going to take another bus, even one with a black driver. I started walking and hitchhiking. That's really when I got to see how people are, up close and personal."

"And, how are they?"

"Either totally cool or totally fucked. Like most truck drivers are cool because they'll pick you up when you're walking alone in the middle of the desert, except some are weird ass motherfuckers who want to jump your bones and have sex with you. "

"But I can tell you, because I know, this country mostly hates black folks. Sometimes I'd get lost and I'd walk down some dirt road to some little house on the jackass prairie and they'd look at me like I was an alien from *Close Encounters* and they'd turn their dog on me, or pull out a gun. In some states, the police would hassle me for hitchhiking, and then the same cops would come back in an hour and hassle me again for walking on the side of the road. They'd try to bust me for being a vagrant, but they couldn't because I still had money, so then they'd ask me who I'd stolen it from. It went on and on. But the worse it got, the more I had to finish. It took me three months. I got beaten up, got robbed, almost got raped twice, and got arrested six times. But I got to L.A. with two hundred dollars and I knew I could live on the street for the rest of my life if I had to. I'm nineteen and I'm strong, and I don't want nothing to do with a shit establishment world that doesn't want me. Fuck them."

"Any good moments on your trip?"

"Colorado was cool. Amazing mountains. Lots of stars in the sky there."

Trent has nothing else to say, so Dwight turns the camera off.

Maggie sips her coffee. "Do you believe him?"

Paul ejects the tape. "Sure. Why not?"

"It just seems like he might be exaggerating," she says. "He's so dramatic."

"It's probably why they put him on the show."

Paul puts the one labeled *Jodi* in the VCR next and hits PLAY.

The screen lights up to reveal a thin and athletic white girl with bleached white hair and pierced ears, pierced nose, pierced eyebrow and pierced tongue. She wears a white ribbed t-shirt through which her nipples show, and the edge of a black tattoo creeps up from between her breasts. She sits on a ratty old red velvet couch and wears dirty army fatigues and combat boots. She lights a cigarette.

On tape, Dwight's voice returns. "Comfortable?"

"Whatever," Jodi answers. She had a deep rough voice for such a small girl.

"Jodi. Can you tell me how you came to be homeless?"

"I ran away from home when I was sixteen. That was three years ago. I ended up in Los Angeles, met some other gutter punk anarchist losers, and I've been here ever since."

"Tell me how that happened."

Jodi sighed, bored, and irritated.

"Ever heard of Willits Park, California?"

"No, I haven't."

"You're lucky. It's this air-conditioned suburban nightmare. All the houses are the same, twisting down these perfect little streets ending in cul-de-sacs. They built the whole town in this big empty field halfway between San Francisco and Napa. It even has a huge plastic sign that lights up at night – Willits Park! – like it's a bowling alley. When I was in school they found out it was built over a toxic oil dump, and everybody realized why so many people had cancer."

"So why did you leave?"

Jodi takes out a Velcro wallet attached to a chain around her waist, pulls out a driver's license and holds it up to the camera. Dwight adjusts the lens. The image that comes into focus is of a pretty, brown-haired, average teenager. It's Jodi.

"This was almost my destiny. Every night I was reading Jean Genet, but during the day I was trapped at the Dairy Queen making Blizzards for all the vanilla cheerleaders and high school wrestlers, fighting the desire to wipe them all out with my Dad's semi-automatic. I had to leave town before I hurt somebody."

"I moved south to San Francisco where I lived in the underground scene for a while, but that town is full of snobs. Even the anarchists and squatters act snobby. 'Oh, we're so cool, we live in an abandoned warehouse in San Francisco!' What's the point? That's why I moved to Los Angeles. This place doesn't care about anything. It just *is*."

"So why do you live like this?" Dwight asks.

"What's wrong with this?"

"You don't want a job, an apartment?"

"What for? So I can commute to some bullshit job every day and then eat fast food every night in front of the TV? I had that growing up. I want to live a *real life*. I want to know what's it's like to be so hungry you have to fight for your food."

"Have you ever been hungry?"

"I'm hungry right now. And I love it!"

Jodi makes a punching motion towards the camera. On the back of her right hand is a tattoo of a big scripted A in a circle, the Anarchy symbol.

The camera shuts off, then comes back on for a second. Jodi and Trent are on screen and she's strangling him. She shouts.

"You ever seen a white woman tongue wrestle a black man?"

She grabs Trent's head and kisses him long and hard. He runs off screen, giggling. "How'd you like that, you damn lemmings? You like to watch us on your TV?" The camera shuts off while she's still shouting.

"She, on the other hand, is way too dramatic," Paul says.

"She'll be a real joy to work with," Maggie says.

Paul ejects the tape. Should we take a break, or keep going?"

"Keep going! This is fun!"

"It's fun for you sitting here. In twelve hours, I'll be living it."

Paul takes out the tape labeled *Ilima* and pops it in the machine.

The bright lights of the L.A. skyscrapers appear on screen. The camera is on a roof and pans across the skyline until it comes to rest on a girl. She struts towards the camera, vamping as if on a catwalk. She comes close to the lens and gives her best haughty model look. She's got perfect brown skin and long black hair. She's wearing a ripped brown leather jacket over a rainbow tube top, and flared blue jeans over white 70s platform pimp shoes. She fakes a karate chop to the camera and laughs.

"Ilima. Tell us how old you are and where you're from."

"My name is Ilima Piilani, I'm Hawaiian and Portuguese, I grew up in Honolulu and I just turned eighteen years old." Ilima smiles; she loves being on camera.

"Why did you come to Los Angeles?"

"To be a model and an actress."

"Hawaii seems like a nice place. Why did you leave?"

"To get away from my stepfather. He was molesting me." Ilima keeps smiling.

"That must have been tough," says Dwight.

"Mom didn't believe me. He did it for two years with me, and three years with my older sister."

"Anything else you want to tell me about that?" asks Dwight.

Ilima smiles, bright and happy. "Nope," she says.

"So how did you end up here?"

"My mom made me join the bell choir in church, except I sucked. I only had to ring one bell once in all the songs, and I always got it wrong. Anyway, the church paid for us to come to the mainland and play Christmas carols in other churches and stay with host families, and when we got to Los Angeles I sneaked out at night and ran away."

"Did you know anybody?"

"Nope. But I meet people really quick."

"Like who?"

"First, I fell in love with Pelle – he's a guitar player from Sweden who shared an apartment in Hollywood with some other guys in his band. Except when nobody liked their music, they blamed me. Pelle made me move out." For the first time, Ilima looks sad. "I met some real jerks after that."

She shrugs and forces the smile back. "But then I met Trent's tribe. Trent and Jodi are like the Mom and Dad and Duncan is like my brother. I feel totally good with them."

"Do you ever talk to your family?"

"I call my Mom sometimes, but she never ever says anything. She just listens on the other end. It's easier for her to blame me."

"What about the modeling?"

"In the back of some papers they list companies looking for models. I went to a couple of them but they all want you to take your clothes off. But one of the guys said he'd do some regular pictures for me to get my portfolio started if I paid him five hundred dollars, so I'm saving money for that. The trouble is, I might need to spend it to get my teeth fixed. It hurts on one side of my mouth, so I chew on the other side."

"Anything else you want to say?"

"I feel lucky. I think good things are going to happen to us, if we stick together."

The camera shuts off and Paul hits eject. Neither of them moves for a full minute.

"I can't believe she actually feels lucky," Maggie says.

"She's better off than she was before. Maybe that's good."

"Paul, the girl's teeth are rotting out of her mouth."

"Hey, I didn't cast her. I just took the job."

"It's exploitation, that's what it is."

Maggie gets up for more coffee. Paul picks up the last tape, labeled *Duncan*.

"You still want to watch this?" Paul pops in the tape. Maggie stays in the kitchen but moves to the doorway to watch. The image that comes up makes her gasp.

"My God, he's gorgeous."

It's the face of a young man with smooth skin except for a thin white scar from his eye to ear – a line that adds character and intrigue to an otherwise perfect face. His eyes are grey and piercing. His black hair is cut close to his head in a crew cut. The camera zooms in and out while Dwight adjusts the iris.

"I don't know, Duncan. There's so little light out here."

Duncan has a smile as calm as Buddha's. Metal creaks loudly. The camera reveals that they're on a fire escape, very high up. Dwight seems nervous – his breath is quick, and it takes a while for the camera to settle. Duncan sits on the edge of the metal railing, an inch away from open air fifty feet up, yet he's comfortable.

"Tell me your name and how old you are."

"I'm Duncan. I'm nineteen, I think."

"You think?"

"I lose track of time."

"How did you end up in Los Angeles?"

Duncan shrugs. "I woke up one day and I was here."

"Where are you from?

"Pretty far off. It would take me awhile to find it again."

"What's your life been like?"

"Nothing special. Like anybody else's." Duncan smiles.

"You can't tell me anything else?" Dwight asks.

"There's not much to tell."

"What about Trent, Jodi and Ilima? Can you talk about them?"

"Trent's in charge. I do what he says. Jodi's funny. She likes to do crazy things. Ilima is a good talker. She talks all night long. Living with them is fun. I like it."

The camera waits, but Duncan just stares and smiles. The metal fire escape creaks and moves an inch down. Dwight gasps and swears.

"This thing is ready to fall, huh?" Duncan laughs, and the camera shuts off.

Paul ejects the tape. "You think he's still gorgeous when he opens his mouth?"

"He's a man of few words."

"Maybe he only knows a few words." Paul sweeps the tapes back in their box.

"I think he's the most interesting of all of them."

Paul stares at her, amazed she's defending him. "He's got nothing to say. What's so intriguing about somebody who's empty?"

"The others never shut up. He's at least got some mystery." Maggie pulls her robe around her, embarrassed. "You find the girl with the bad teeth attractive, admit it."

"This is a stupid conversation."

Paul turns the TV off. It's ten a.m. They only have another eight hours together before he must be at work. He wishes the eight hours would never end, and at the same time he wishes they were already over. Maggie moves closer.

"How busy is this job going to keep you?"

"My guess is I'll be lucky to have a day off."

"Looks like we're still both 'paying our dues,'" she says.

Paul hates that phrase. *Paying your dues* means you're getting ripped off, and the only thing you gain is knowing *how* they're taking advantage of you, so you can either avoid it the next time or use it yourself on someone else. Paul has learned this lesson many times, but here he is, ready to 'pay his dues' yet again.

"We'll be okay."

"Will we?" she asks.

Her eyes burn into him. He almost got away, but with one small question she brings the big question back in the room. After two months of living together, during which they fought often and rarely made love, she wants him to decide their future. A twinge in his gut tells him they won't be together in six months, but he ignores it.

"I think so. I hope so," he offers.

She narrows her eyes at him. If he had answered "yes," she would've jumped into his arms, and he would've carried her right back to the couch and thrown the damn tapes across the room and opened her robe one last time before his new crazy job started.

"Fine. I'll guess we'll see."

CHAPTER 8

P aul stares out the window as the bus flies down Wilshire, across Western, and into the buzzing neon lights of Koreatown. He locked his car in Maggie's garage and changed the outgoing message on her answering machine to tell the creditors that he is "on location" for six weeks, which isn't a lie considering how little time he'll have off.

They cross Alameda Boulevard into no-man's land and he rings the "stop requested" bell. He is the only person left on the bus.

"You sure you know where you're going?" the driver asks.

"I got an address. TV location." Paul steps onto the pavement.

The driver smiles. "Have fun slumming." The pneumatic doors hiss shut, and Paul is left standing in a cloud of diesel dust.

Paul looks around. The neighborhood is so empty there aren't even cars on the street. It's just past nightfall and the lights of the skyscrapers behind him glow orange. He hears the distant rumbling of the freeway, the ubiquitous noise of Los Angeles. He spots the building a block away, a three-story cement warehouse with a faded mug of beer stenciled on the side: the abandoned brewery. He walks over.

A solitary white panel van is parked across the street, so he knocks on the door. A screaming face with a gun appears at the window.

"Get away from van!"

Paul steps back, his hands in the air. "I'm Paul! I'm the new audio guy!"

The van's back door flies open and spits out a short muscular man who grabs Paul's hand. He is in his mid-40s, in great shape, with a full head of black hair. "Victor Nadyze," he says with a Russian accent.

"Cameraman. Sorry about gun. It's to scare off the poor crazy people."

"Is Dwight around?"

"He went to get us food. The kids are still asleep."

Paul looks up at the three-floor cement building. It's dark, and all the doors and ground floor windows are boarded over. "Do they really live in there?"

"It's not that bad. Where I come from some people live much worse. Many times, they freeze to death in winter, the conditions are so terrible."

Victor spits and shakes his head at the memory, begging Paul to ask the question. "Where in Russia are you from?" Paul asks.

"Moscow. But I'm here fifteen years. I defect from Afghanistan."

Paul waits to see if Victor will now ask a question about him. Nothing.

"Were you a soldier, Victor?" Paul asks, to keep the conversation going.

"I was in Soviet Army, Special Forces. I served five years in mountains outside Kabul." He looks Paul hard in the eye, demanding respect. "Near the end, we were losing badly. Our battalion was surrounded and couldn't retreat, so I abandoned struggle and sneaked into Kabul alone at night. Because I was officer, I knew I could trade information with CIA for freedom. But I had to find the Americans first, before Mujahedeen found me."

Paul smiles and nods while Victor studies him with blank eyes, which makes Paul wonder where Victor put his gun. Then Paul feels the warm summer wind on his face and he can smell jasmine even in the heart of downtown, standing on an abandoned street at sunset with an angry Russian war veteran. *Another movie moment*. He files it away.

The wind blows up a dust tornado. A trash can fire flickers on a corner a few blocks down and Paul can see people creeping on a warehouse roof a few hundred yards away. The night people are coming out. Maybe it's a good thing that Victor and his gun are around.

"How did you end up on this project, Victor?" Paul asks.

"I started first doing paparazzi. I was the best. You remember Cher?"

"Sure do. Very talented actress."

"For a year I follow her, never stopping, using my military training to track her, to hide, and take photos. Her boyfriend tried to run me down in her Ferrari and crashed the car. Those were my best pictures." He pulls up his t-shirt to reveal a tattoo of Cher from *Moonstruck* on his shoulder. "Cher made me a lot of money. Now I shoot video."

Big Andy's truck rounds the corner and stops.

"That's my gear. I'll be right back," Paul says, glad to be able to walk away.

Andy and Paul meet at the tailgate and dab fists. "Nice buzz cut," Andy says. "The scar makes you look mean."

"I can't complain. It helped me get the job."

Andy motions towards Victor, who is glaring at them. "Who's the psycho?"

"The cameraman. I think he killed the last audio guy."

Andy opens a silver carrying case and pulls out the gear – black graphite microphones, cables, a boom pole, headphones, transmitters, tiny radio microphones batteries, and a small metal box with a lot of knobs – the mixer that controls everything.

Then out comes the blue bag that will hold all of it. Paul watches as each piece of gear fits into its own Velcro spot in the bag, with slots left over for nine-volt batteries, black Sharpie pens, a micro-tool kit, a tiny metal flashlight, sticky tape in black, white, green, red and grey, and an extra set of stereo headphones. Then Andy hands Paul his harness: a shoulder-to-waist contraption that will hold the bag in place across Paul's hips and chest. This leaves his two hands free, so he can hold the boom pole.

"This is all your gear, plus the metal case," Andy explains.

Paul blinks at it all, unable to move. "I hope you're getting a good rate on this stuff because it'll be completely ruined by the time I'm done with it."

Andy pushes the bag towards him. "We're an hour early. Just practice taking it apart and putting it together a dozen times. You'll be fine."

Andy is right. It's not that different than what he does for Andy in the mixing studio, only it's small and compact and runs on batteries.

Paul puts on the harness and attaches the blue bag. He feels himself gain thirty pounds. He tries extending the boom pole and gets tangled in his own wires, then the bag shifts slightly and pitches him forward into the street. Andy catches him. Paul glances at Victor, who shakes his head and goes back into the van.

"In ten hours, you'll be an expert."

"I'm supposed to be an expert already. They think we own this rig together."

Paul takes all the gear off and lays it on the tailgate. He shakes, mostly from fear.

"I have to get a hat," he lies. "Without any hair, I'm freezing out here."

Andy sees through it. "Relax. You've shot enough video to know what the audio guy does. Just get the sound and stay out of the cameraman's way. If you get good sound on tape, no one notices you. The minute you screw up, that's when it's all your fault," he warns. "And when in doubt, fake it. You know more than they do, remember that."

"I'll remember."

Andy pulls out his keys, ready to go. "Are you going to be okay?"

"I'll be cool. Just wear your pager, please."

"I'm available, 24/7." Paul and Andy punch fists and Andy climbs in his truck and drives away, leaving Paul alone with gear worth thousands of dollars.

Paul walks back over to the white panel van. Victor opens the back door and waves for Paul to come look. Inside are monitors, cameras, a microwave transmitter and receiver, carpeted wooden shelves stacked with replacement parts, camping chairs, a couple of coolers and a foam mattress. Paul wonders if Victor lives in there.

Paul then spots Dwight from a block away, carrying two paper sacks. Head held high, he walks with firm purpose, telegraphing his point: others might drive, but he *walks* in Los Angeles, and he gets the food himself. And he buys his own lunch. No assistant, no catering, no big production, no *bullshit*. Dwight keeps his crew small, and does it all himself, because he's an artist. He arrives and nods at Paul.

"Good evening. We have about ten minutes to fuel up before we go in. I hope you like burritos." He hands Paul his dinner.

"Before we start, let's go over a few of the rules," Dwight says between wolf-size bites. "First, I'm a purist when it comes to documentaries. I'm the first to admit that we alter 'reality' the moment we walk into a room with a camera, but my goal is to alter it as little as possible."

"I appreciate that," Paul says in mid chew. They are all rushing through their meal in five minutes. Does he eat every meal this way?

"We're like wildlife documentary filmmakers in the bush. If our behavior is systematic and repetitive, then the animals we're filming grow acclimated to our presence and return to how they naturally behave. That's true with lions, elephant seals, bears and humans. Our goal is to become a regular, predictable part of their lives. Right, Victor?"

Paul looks over at Victor. The Russian preps his camera gear in total concentration. Paul imagines him prepping his weapons with the same intensity, just before tumbling out of some mud hut and sweeping down upon a band of unsuspecting Afghans. Victor starts barking back the rules, his eyes never leaving his work.

"The rules are – one: we never talk to cast. Two: we never display emotion in front of cast. Three: we must wear dark neutral clothing.

Four: we shoot four thirty-minute tapes then take a ten-minute break. During the break, we retreat to neutral area where we change batteries, check gear, and drink water. There is Porta-Potty on side of building for us, but only us. Five: we only eat during meal breaks, which are every six hours. There is no snacking, and no showing food or drinks to cast. Six: we never give money, even show money, to cast." Victor slams a thirty-minute tape into the camera and stands up. Locked and loaded, ready for battle. Paul is surprised that Victor didn't salute.

Dwight smiles, proud of his soldier. "Any questions?"

"Where will you be?" Paul asks.

"In the van." Dwight points to a large white baton strapped to the side of Victor's camera – a microwave transmitter. "This sends the TV signal to the van, where I see everything Victor shoots. Victor wears a walkie-talkie with a headset, so I can tell him what to shoot. Your job is to get the audio and to watch Victor. Stay out of his way, and any direction from me will come through him."

A buzz came from inside the open van. Victor walks over and turns up the volume on a speaker. A voice came through: "Come on, Trent! You owe me those smokes!"

"Jodi's awake," Dwight says.

"Where's that coming from?" Paul asks.

"I hid microphones inside, to hear them." Victor says.

Paul looks at the two men. Dwight is the general, and Victor is his soldier of fortune. They are in synch, and Paul isn't.

"Another thing," Dwight says. "You're new and they'll notice you and talk about you. Just follow the rules and it will pass." Dwight looks at his watch. "Let's move."

Dwight steps into the back of the van and crouches down next to the monitors. How can he direct like that? Paul wonders. Victor shuts and locks the back door of the van, lifts the camera on his shoulder and darts across the street. Paul scrambles to gather his gear, tripping over his own boom cable as he chases after him.

Paul sees no way to get inside the old building – every opening is nailed shut. But there is a fire escape. Victor puts his camera down, steps back and then runs and hits the wall high with his shoe, gaining just enough height to catch a dangling cord tied to the last step of the metal stairs. He cantilevers the ladder down to the ground, pulling the staircase into range.

The metal structure sways under Paul's feet. Five, maybe six bolts prevent the whole structure from shearing away from the building like ice off a glacier. Paul remembers how nervous Dwight had been on the fire escape during Duncan's interview, and how calm and collected Duncan seemed.

At the first landing, Victor lifts the ladder back up, then pushes at the plywood sheet covering the first window. It swings open, revealing a dark cement hallway inside.

Paul is excited, and it surprises him. He hasn't felt this kind of exhilaration in a long time, especially not during the grind of the last year. It's a rush, like how he felt when he was in that speed metal band in college and they first walked out on stage, or at his first film festival just as the lights dimmed. Or when he first made love with Maggie, when their clothes came off and they both knew there was no going back. The rush means that he is on the edge, and either great things or dreadful things are about to happen, and he doesn't know which. That edge is where he is now, and it's raw and glorious, and full of the thrill of the new. He realizes how much he misses it.

"You ready?" Victor asks. Paul nods and they step through.

CHAPTER 9

They creep through the first room and through a dark cement hallway. "Careful where you walk," Victor whispers. "There's broken glass and water everywhere."

They reach the vast main room of the brewery, which has six metal circles on the floor where the vats once were. Paul looks up and sees moonlight seeping through the greasy windows high above. A maze of pipes is barely visible in the darkness.

They turn a corner into another cement hallway and Paul gets smacked in the face by the stale smell of sweat, beer and urine. They creep towards a light in a doorway. It's a glowing light bulb hanging in the first of four storage rooms, which are the smallest and warmest spaces in the brewery, and the best place to set up house. Paul is surprised there is electricity and wonders if the kids found a rare outlet that still works or whether the production rigged it for them.

The camera spots Jodi first, lying on the ratty red sofa and popping a zit in the peach fuzz of her underarm hair. She looks up.

"Hollywood's back. Everyone put their makeup on."

Trent emerges from a dark hallway, carrying a bowl of fire – a plastic bowl filled with candle wax, wood, cloth and kerosene and all set ablaze. He puts it on a ledge close to a window. He holds up a finger and recites a poem:

"Burn bright, good light,

Bring us warmth, give us sight,

Destroy the dark and make things right."

Victor jabs Paul in the ribs and points at his ear. Victor is shooting but Paul isn't giving him any audio. Paul extends his boom pole and aims the microphone towards Jodi.

"Look! It's a new guy! Hey new guy!"

They spin towards the voice – it's Ilima. She stares right into the lens and croons.

"Do me, babe-bay, do me, babe-bay," She reaches for the microphone, but Paul raises his boom out of her reach. She jumps for it, but can't reach very high in her tight jeans and platform shoes. Yet she keeps jumping and laughing, like an exuberant five-year-old leaping for candy.

"Come on, new guy. I just want to sing. Let me sing!" Paul doesn't know what to do; he's been in the room less than a minute and all the attention is on him. Victor keeps shooting. She finally stops and gasps for breath. She starts to cough, a deep bronchial hawking that brings up heavy phlegm. Ilima spits and readjusts her breasts in her tube top and walks away.

Victor moves to the corner for a wide shot and Paul finally gets a look at the whole room. The ratty red velvet sofa from the casting video is pushed against a wall spattered with red and white paint. Two wooden pallets covered with yellowed newspapers and old clothes are their beds, and a half-dozen hard plastic buckets double both as stools and containers, depending on which end is up.

Trent sits on one of the pallets eating cold French fries out of a paper bag. Ilima picks up a big blue felt tip marker and writes her name on the wall a dozen times. Jodi digs through the sofa cushions until she finds the butt end of a cigarette and lights up. No one speaks.

Paul can only hear the audio in his own headphones from the microphones the kids are wearing and from the boom he holds. Victor nods, as if listening to an invisible voice. Dwight must be directing him. Victor shoots wide shots ... he circles around each kid slowly ... he pans from one to the other ... he gets on his knees and shoots their faces from below ... he stands on the windowsill and frames the lightbulb in the shot and aims down on them from above ... he goes out into the hallway and shoots through the open door, as if spying on them from another room ... he shoots their hands moving, their shoes tapping, and extreme close-ups of their pupils dilating.

During all this shooting, the kids do nothing.

So, Paul gets the sounds of doing nothing: Jodi sucking in the last bit of tobacco in her cigarette butt ... Ilima's felt tip pen squeaking against the cool cement ... Trent scraping the last bit of cold French fries against the ketchup in the bottom of a paper bag.

"I need cigarettes," Jodi complains, breaking the silence. "And beer."

"Then go get it," Trent answers. "You got legs."

"I want to get a dog," Ilima says.

"A dog will stink up the place," Trent says.

"It already stinks," Jodi counters.

"We're hungry enough. I don't want to worry about feeding a dog too," Trent says.

"Then I want my own room," Ilima says.

"When we get enough furniture, you'll get your own room," Trent says.

A banging noise comes from the hallway. Victor aims towards the open door. Out of the darkness steps Duncan. The light shines off his dirty crewcut, and he has a big smile on his face. He also has a fresh black bruise on his left cheek. He is the only one of the four who looks as big in real life as he does on tape, Paul thinks.

Duncan holds up a suitcase. "Look what I found," he says, holding it straight out. His knuckles are raw and bloody.

The others gather around. Paul extends his boom as Victor moves his camera closer. Duncan unzips the brown vinyl suitcase and flips open the top. Eight hands shoot inside, grabbing white t-shirts, big boxer underwear and wide grey trousers.

"Clown pants!" Jodi shouts. "I'll wear these!"

They rummage through their new treasures. The girls split up the razors and shaving cream. The boys find dirty magazines at the bottom and tear them open, cooing at the naked skin. Last of all, Ilima finds a deck of cards in one of the side pockets.

"We can play Hearts!" she yells. "I loved playing Hearts when I was little.""

Jodi spots a hidden zippered pocket on the inside of the open suitcase. Victor moves in for a close-up and Jodi slows down and turns sideways, so he can get his shot of the open suitcase. She carefully unzips the pocket, reaches inside and pulls out a wad of money. "We're rich!" she says, holding it up.

"Good work, Duncan" Trent says. "Excellent."

Duncan moves away from the group and sits on the couch, smiling.

Jodi counts out the wad of money, and it's all one-dollar bills. "Twenty-five dollars. Not much, but it's enough for pancakes for a while." Jodi hands Trent the money.

"Duncan, where did you find it?" Ilima asks.

"Find what?" he asks from the couch.

"This suitcase," Jodi says.

"In the bathroom at the train station."

"An effective redistribution of the wealth. I like it," Trent says.

"Who'd you steal it from?" Jodi asks.

Duncan blinks; he doesn't understand the question.

"You stole it, Duncan," Jodi explains. "Suitcases don't just sit there, it belonged to somebody who was taking a train trip."

Duncan shifts. "It was just sitting there in the bathroom, so I took it, when this fat guy knocked me down in the parking lot and we started fighting. I guess it was his."

His squat mates laugh. Ilima opens the playing cards and she and Jodi play Hearts while Duncan watches. Trent reads. Victor shoots this for an hour until Jodi finally speaks.

"I need cigarettes," she declares again, and Victor and Paul follow her out of the room, down a short hall filled with metal and trash, and into what was once an office. Burning votive candles illuminate a stained mattress surrounded by magazines, clothes, paper and trash. It's not that different than any teenager's room, Paul thinks.

Jodi finds her prize – a pack of Kool Menthol cigarettes. She returns to the main room and lights one up, blowing smoke toward the ceiling. Ilima starts coughing.

Her coughs last a full minute, until she brings up a chunk of phlegm that she spits in the corner. Trent and Jodi look at each other and shrug.

"We need more fire, it's getting dark in here," Trent says.

"On it." Duncan jumps off the couch and Victor backpedals to get a moving shot of him, then pausing to shoot over Duncan's shoulder as he digs through a corner trash pile. He finds a smoke-blackened Mason jar with its own cloth, wax and kerosene mix. Victor then follows him over to the windowsill where the bowl of fire is already burning.

Victor moves close, capturing Duncan's face backlit in the yellow flames. Duncan wraps his hand with a strip of rag then picks up the fiery bowl and pours a layer of the burning mess into the Mason jar. The mixture lights up fast. Duncan then pours fire from one container to the other, playing mad scientist.

"Check this out," he calls to his squat mates.

He blows out the fire in the bowl, tests the still hot mixture with his fingers, then plunges his whole hand in the mess. When he pulls his hand out, it looks like he's wearing a black glove of greasy wax. He jumps and dances and blows air on it. Victor gets a shot of the steam rising off the black glove while Paul gets the sound of the wax hissing as it dries on Duncan's flesh. Duncan then holds his black hand up high for all to see, then passes it through the flames in the Mason jar. His hand lights up like a candle.

Trent and Ilima rush forward, but Duncan keeps them back with a sweep of his fiery hand. The fire burns the exterior wax, but it doesn't quite reach his pink flesh, so he's not in pain yet. He parades around the room like the Statue of Liberty, his hand ablaze, singing his rendition of an army march. Victor slides in front of him and walks backward to get a face shot, then follows behind him for an over-the-shoulder shot.

"Stop it, Duncan," Trent says.

"Please, stop, Duncan. Please," Ilima begs.

Jodi takes another drag of her cigarette and shakes her head. "Idiot," she mutters.

Duncan's face contorts, his singing turns to shouting, and he flings his hand down hard, throwing most of the burning wax off his hand and onto the floor. He then pours half a can of flat beer over his red skin, flexing his fingers.

"That was the last of the beer, you moron," Jodi mutters.

Trent walks around the room stomping out small burning pools of wax left on the floor. "Don't do that shit anymore, Duncan," he warns, poking Duncan in the chest. "I don't want to die in a squat fire."

Duncan pouts and sits back on the couch, his chin on his chest.

"You want to play?" Ilima asks, holding up the deck of cards.

Duncan shakes his head like a little kid.

"We could teach you. It's easy."

Again, Duncan shakes his head.

The kids go back to playing their cards.

"I saw a stray dog that lives close to the river. I think she had puppies," Ilima says, which makes Trent sigh.

Victor shoots another two tapes of them playing cards. Jodi smokes four more cigarettes, Ilima keeps coughing and talking about dogs, and Trent counts a pile of pennies on the floor. He seems to have forgotten about the wad of dollar bills in his pocket.

Paul's neck and back ache. Working audio is much tougher than shooting; he can at least rest a camera on his shoulder, but he must hold the boom pole over his head using all muscle power, and spasms ripples up his back and down his arms, making the boom shake. No one notices, except Duncan.

Duncan stares at the boom vibrating like a peppershaker over his head, then looks up at Paul and smiles. Paul smiles back and tries to steady himself but can't.

"Hey, the new guy has a scar," he announces to the room.

"We're supposed to be ignoring them," Jodi reminds him.

"But he's got a scar, like me. Except his is on the back of his head and mine is on my face. What's your name?" Duncan asks.

Suddenly, there is no audio. Paul looks down – his batteries are dead. Victor stops the camera and pulls him out of the room and back towards the fire escape.

"We break for ten minutes."

"Thank God. My back is killing me."

Victor tugs open the plywood door, undoes the cord and lets the fire escape sweep to the ground. Dwight is waiting for them at the bottom and gets right in Paul's face. "I thought you knew what you were doing," he hisses, revealing a side of him that Paul never saw during his interview in the sleek office.

"I do. It's a new situation, and these are new batteries –"

"Don't bullshit me. Your boom volume is way too loud, then too low."

"It's first night jitters," Paul says. He turns to Victor. "I'm keeping up, right?"

Victor shakes his head. "Wrong. You bump me, then when I move, you three steps behind. You either in my way or never there."

"I'm trying. But they're doing nothing in there, and we're shooting all of it."

"This is the show. Get used to it," Dwight says. "And what are you doing to Duncan?"

"Nothing. I have no idea why he's obsessing over me."

"You're doing *something*. Figure out what it is and stop it or I'll pull you out and take that boom and go in myself," Dwight warns.

"You're not touching this gear," Paul shoots right back. "If you want to pull me, then do it and I'll take my rig and go home. Find someone else."

Dwight stares at Paul, frozen, then walks back across the street to the van. Victor obediently follows. Paul called his bluff and now Paul knows just how badly Dwight needs him, but he also sees how that can easily make Dwight hate him.

Paul takes off his audio rig and changes all his batteries. His wet shirt clings to his back and the cool breeze makes him shiver. Fuck him, Paul thinks. He knew he'd get a drubbing the first night, but not this bad. And over what? Some dumb kids squatting in an abandoned brewery?

Paul carries his rig around the building and finds the Porta Potty. The stench inside is so revolting that he goes back outside and marks the wall instead, a long slow pee that gives him his only sense of relief so far tonight. He zips himself up and steps back around the building, where Victor waits for him with water and a granola bar.

"He yelled at me all my first week, then stopped. He will stop with you too."

He hopes Victor is right; he doesn't want to spend six weeks with a boss who is an absolute dick, no matter how famous a filmmaker he is.

Dwight sticks his head out of the van. "They're on the move! Let's go!"

Paul stuffs the granola bar in his mouth and wets it with a swig of water. Victor grabs his camera and is already halfway across the street before Paul even picks up his rig. He glances at his watch – he'd been outside six minutes.

CHAPTER 10

D wight keeps yelling. "I want radio mikes on Trent and Jodi!" They dash back up the fire escape and back into the building. Paul rifles through his bag as he runs, finds the two radio microphone packages, then trips and falls to his knees. Victor keeps running.

Victor is already rolling tape when Paul gets back to the small storage rooms where they live. Jodi, Duncan and Ilima hand Trent all their coins and crumpled dollar bills for him to count.

"We have nine dollars, along with bus fare."

"We need more than this if we're going to get shit-faced," Jodi complains.

"It's enough for beer," Trent counters. He doesn't offer up the twenty-five dollars Trent took from the suitcase, Paul notices, and no one challenges him

"We'll spange for change on Hollywood Boulevard," Trent says.

Ilima moans. "It's so far away! And the Hollywood gutter punks have the best corners already picked out. We're just going to get into a fight."

"Stay here then," Trent says. "We'll bring some back."

They all look at her. Ilima coughs and pulls her jacket around her. Victor pushes in tight for a close-up on her face. She looks afraid. "Okay, I'll come."

The kids take out pocket lighters and light a path down a staircase strewn with a moonlit carpet of broken glass. The kids have their own entrance through a steel door with a padlock and Trent has the key. They step through, lock up their home again, and start walking, with Victor doing his camera dance alongside. Dwight drives the white van, trailing them. Paul runs alongside, holding his boom aloft while mixing the audio. We must look like a weird circus, Paul thinks.

During the day, this area past downtown Los Angeles hides eleven thousand homeless men, women and children. They pass hundreds of cardboard boxes, each one home to another homeless person. Every two hundred yards is a rusted oil drum with a wood fire, and a dozen men and women gather around it.

On every block, a homeless man approaches – either slow and shy, asking for help, or loud and rude, insisting that they give him a job or some cash. Each time Victor pauses his camera, pulls his gun from his pants and points it at the man. "I kill you!"

"Crazy Russian man, relax," one man says. "We're just being friendly."

The kids reach the subway station and stop, as if on cue. Victor whispers into the boom microphone so Paul can hear him. "This is when we put microphones on them."

Paul approaches Trent and Jodi with the radio microphones. Neither make eye contact with him but understand his lowly task – they just raise their arms, so he can attach the microphones to their collars, then snake the lines through their shirts and plug them into transmitters the size of a deck of cards. He either slides their transmitter into their pocket or he clips it to their belt.

"One two three four five," they mutter. Paul adjusts their volumes and nods at them, and like bored celebrities they all sigh and walk into the station.

Dwight honks from the van and drives away.

Victor takes the camera off his shoulder and motions for Paul to follow him down the subway stairs. "Dwight will meet us at Hollywood station. We are not allowed to shoot here," Victor whispers, "but I will grab shots from my hip so keep power up. Just listen to radio mics."

The kids blend in with the rest of humanity traveling the downtown trains at night, they just seem a little dirtier. Duncan points to the scar on his face, and then points to Paul's head and gives him a big thumbs-up sign. Paul smiles and gives him the thumbs-up back. Why not? Dwight is somewhere forty feet above them, racing up Western Avenue trying to beat the train.

"What's your name?" Duncan moves his mouth in a whisper.

Paul writes his name on his palm with a Sharpie and holds it up for Duncan to see. Duncan stares at it and shrugs. Either Duncan is blind, or the kid can't read.

An hour later they are on Hollywood Boulevard across the street from Mann's Chinese Theater, where Paul sliced his head open just two days earlier, the accident that helped him get this job. It already seems like a year ago. The street is crowded with Hollywood punks, night-clubbers and tourists taking snapshots of the boulevard. The kids disappear into the crowd. Victor steps to the curb and Paul falls in place behind him.

Paul hears Victor's headset crackle and sees Dwight in the white van fifty yards away. "Get ready, the kids are about to do something," Victor says.

Paul turns up their radio mics. They are close by. He then spots Trent and Duncan walking down the sidewalk from opposite ends. They bump shoulders directly in front of a group of tourists.

"Watch where you're going, you black bastard," Duncan says.

"Shut your mouth, you white Nazi. Or I'll shut it for you," Trent pushes him.

They attack one another, swinging their fists at each other's faces with full force, each ducking just in time to take the blows in the chest and the back of the head.

A crowd gathers, cameras flashing. Victor circles the duo, pushing close, then retreating just before a punch nails him— it's clear that he has shot this before and knows their precise choreography.

Paul extends his boom and catches whispers from the crowd: "Is this real? I think it is....no, look at the camera, it's a TV show ... but they're really hitting each other..."

Dwight rushes around the corner with his headset on, looking at a small TV monitor in his hand, already barking instructions to Victor. A subset of tourists breaks off from the crowd to surround Dwight and watch him bark into his headset. He is now "the show."

"White punk ass mother fucker!" Trent screams and tackles Duncan to the sidewalk. Trent rubs Duncan's face into the pavement and then bites him hard on the shoulder. Duncan screams. If this is a put-on, Paul is impressed.

Trent and Duncan jump to their feet, their arms and faces red with scrapes.

"Black bastard! You fucked my sister!"

Duncan takes a step back and swings his foot at Trent's groin with full force. Trent puts out his hands to block the kick, and at the last moment Duncan flattens the arch of his foot, so his boot connects only with Trent's cupped hands, right at crotch level. But the smack is loud and lifts Trent off the ground. He collapses to the sidewalk groaning. The crowd gasps. Jodi rushes forward, tears in her eyes, and gets on her knees and hugs Trent.

The crowd moves closer. Jodi cradles Trent's head, pauses for a beat, sniffs, waits for Victor to fall into place with his camera, then stares at Duncan with tears running down her face. "Stop fighting! I love him, Carl! I'm going to have his baby! And you're going to have a nephew!" Jodi screams at Duncan.

Victor swings his camera around and gets Duncan in frame for his answer. Duncan falls to his knees, weeping. Huge sobs wrack his body as snot runs in a stream from his nose. "Please, Diane ... Carl ... you're my only family! Forgive me! I won't stand in the way of your love!"

Paul is shocked by what a good actor he is. Duncan's words are cheesy, but the moment feels real. The crowd falls silent, until you can only hear the traffic on Hollywood Boulevard and the helicopters overhead. Paul spots two tourist women in velour jumpsuits wiping away tears.

Trent jumps up, throws out his arms and bows. Ilima rushes in and helps Jodi and Duncan to their feet, so all four can bow together. The crowd groans and laughs and then applauds, especially for Duncan. Trent takes off his cap and walks into the crowd.

"Donations? Just some street kids trying to make it in Hollywood. Donations?"

Coins and dollar bills go into his hat, as tourists slap them on the back. "You guys are great...you should be on TV...that was amazing."

The crowd moves on. Paul holds the boom high as Victor pushes in for a shot of Trent counting out the money: thirty dollars.

"Liquor Store!" Jodi yells, and off they go, running down Hollywood Boulevard with Victor and Paul dashing alongside, while Dwight sprints on the other side of the street, his face stuck in his handheld TV monitor while muttering commands into his walkie-talkie.

They find a liquor store and three minutes later the kids are in an alley ripping cans out of a twelve-pack and chugging beer as fast as they can swallow. After two cans, Ilima starts coughing. She pulls her jacket tight around her while everyone watches and waits for the spell to pass. Her face turns grey for a minute before turning pink again. "I'm hungry," she says.

They end up at the International House of Pancakes on Sunset Boulevard. No one awake at 2 a.m. cares about smoking laws, so Trent and Jodi light up cigarette after cigarette, crushing the butts into the remnants of their strawberry pancakes. Duncan empties sugar packets into his mouth while Ilima counts their remaining money on the table. "We got nineteen dollars."

"We need ten for the pancakes and need five to get back to the vats. That leaves us four dollars to waste," Trent says.

Jodi snaps her fingers over her head. "More beer then!"

"We're already tanked, I need a bag of speed to back this up. I don't want to ride the fucking subway back downtown unless I'm high," Trent complains.

"We don't have the money for speed," Jodi says.

They pick at their pancakes and argue for ten minutes over whether to get beer or speed, then hit a lull, then argue again for another ten minutes.

Dwight sits five booths down watching on his monitor, giving Victor instructions. Paul is so hungry that even the smashed-up pancakes and cigarette butts look good, but he doesn't dare eat anything. Food at this point would just make him sleepier than he already is. The kids' argument enters its fifth cycle about beer versus speed, while Victor shoots close-ups, pans, and over-the-shoulder shots. Why were they even shooting this? This is nowhere as interesting as their fight on Hollywood Boulevard, Paul thinks. The fight on the street and Duncan parading with his hand on fire were the best moments of the night.

"Let's get some vodka and chocolate milk," Trent says.

"I want some weed," Ilima says. Her cough returns, and she hacks up crud.

"Let's just choke each other until we pass out. That gets us high and it's free," Duncan says. Jodi shakes her head and punches him.

Victor motions "cut" to Paul and they step away for their break. They take off their gear and slide down in the booth next to Dwight.

"This is same thing they did last Saturday night," Victor moans.

"Exactly," Dwight explains. "This is their routine. That's the point. Don't worry, it'll all become clear in the edit bay," Dwight says. He turns to Paul. "I was out of audio range when I was driving the van and catching up. What did they talk about?"

"Ilima wants to go home and go to sleep, but Trent wants to do something crazy for the cameras."

Victor spits on the floor. "That is because Trent wants own TV series."

Dwight points his finger in Victor's face. "No judgment, stay neutral."

Victor growls but drops his eyes. He's insane, but he follows the chain of command, which is why Dwight likes him. That, and the fact that he can work nonstop for eight days straight.

Paul neglects to tell Dwight that while Dwight was out of range they also talked about him, the new guy. They all agreed they liked Paul better than the last audio guy. At least they knew his name. Paul curls his hand to hide his name inked onto his palm.

Paul glances back and sees bills flashing at the kids' table and hears a slight change in the tone of Trent's voice. He slides the headphones back on.

"You had this all along? Why didn't you say anything?" Trent asks.

"I dunno," Duncan says. "I was saving it for something for myself."

"All money is tribal money," Trent says, and takes Duncan's cash.

Paul turns to Dwight. "Duncan just gave Trent some money, at least twenty dollars."

The kids rise out of their chairs. Victor slams in a new beta tape, runs out the front door and spins around to get a shot of the exterior as the kids leave the restaurant. Paul makes it out the door ten steps ahead of the kids and clears Victor's frame just in time.

The kids stagger down the street, wasted as much from exhaustion as liquor. Paul gets the feeling that if the camera crew broke for the night the kids would go home, but Trent pulls them along, creating the show. The streets are empty at this hour, so Dwight can easily trail the whole group in the white van, driving with one hand while directing via walkie-talkie with the other.

They buy four big bottles of beer and then find a dealer outside an after-hours punk club in an alley off Virgil Street, who sells them a white powder he assures them is straight crystal meth. Ilima, Duncan and Jodi snort their share, but Trent wants to smoke his. Victor gets a tight shot as Trent cuts open a cigarette with his pocketknife, dribbles in the powder, then rolls it up like a joint and lights up. Soon everyone's pupils shrink to pinpoints as they get giggly and happy, wide-awake and drunk. They drink the rest of their beers like water.

"Come on," Trent says. "Let's go on a hike."

It's 4 a.m. as Trent leads the group above Sunset Boulevard and into the Hollywood Hills. Victor and Paul run ahead, their gear bouncing off their shoulders and hips, trying to get far enough ahead of them to get a decent shot while Dwight heads far up the street past everyone, parks the van and hops out to meet them.

Paul has moved through four stages of exhaustion. First, his muscles cramped up and he got the sweats, then he got sleepy and could barely keep his eyes open, then he got so hungry that he got the dry-heaves, and now he is floating. The feeling is pleasant; Paul figures it's like what wounded men go through just before dying.

Paul sees no change in Victor, however. He is just as manic as when they met at sunset, and they'd been going almost ten hours without a decent break. Dwight's focus doesn't waver either, no matter how meaningless and mundane the conversation is. Paul can't see doing this night after night and being able to stay alive.

Jodi drains her beer bottle and tosses it down the hill, watching it smash into the empty street. The others do the same, making it rain glass. Dogs start barking. As they climb higher so do the prices of the homes and the parked cars they pass. Bougainvillea bushes and palm and eucalyptus trees make a thick fragrant canopy on the narrow streets. They are in near darkness, the only light coming from hazy porch lights in the early morning fog. There is no extraneous city noise – even the distant highway hiss is absent at this early hour. Ilima starts singing a Hawaiian song, slow and lilting, like a hymn. The others listen to its mournfulness, letting it sink in, and use its rhythm to beat out the steps of their slow climb. They seem like tired, lonely, exhausted kids.

Dwight appears with his monitor. Paul can't hear his voice because he's wearing headphones, but he can see him mouth the word "light." Victor snaps on the lamp attached to the top of his camera and it sends out a harsh beam that makes the four kids look like criminals in a spotlight.

Their behavior changes with the flick of that switch. Ilima stops singing and lights up a cigarette instead, and so does Jodi. Trent pulls on car door handles, seeing if any cars will open. With the camera light on, they are hip homeless youth again. Trent grabs at a Mercedes and the car alarm goes off, and they all run off, laughing. Ilima's illness makes her laughter sound deep like a man's, which makes everyone laugh even louder.

Jodi dashes over to a row of garbage bins. It's a garbage day and each house has a big blue bin for recycling alongside the black garbage bin. Jodi walks into Victor's pool of light and leads him over to a blue bin and flips the top – inside is glass, paper, and aluminum. "Time to get to work. We need empty garbage bags."

Trent tosses open a garbage bin, yanks out some full trash bags and empties their contents on the ground. Duncan does the same at the next house down. Now each of them has an empty garbage bag. They dig through the blue recycling bins next, and fill their empty garbage bags with glass bottles and aluminum cans.

"I hate doing this," Ilima says. "This is what *real* homeless people do."

Duncan is the most aggressive, tipping over entire bins with a clatter and then scouring through the mess for cans and glass. Dwight darts up and down the street, whispering into his walkie-talkie. Victor pushes close, lighting the ground so Duncan can grab the cans and bottles before they roll away. Sweat stains cover Duncan's back and the tangy stench of his body odor is overwhelming. All four of them have it – they are in the middle of their meth speed high and the chemicals are oozing out of every pore.

"Get the fuck out of those bins!"

Victor hangs back, getting only the man's silhouette against his garage light. He is in pajamas and a robe.

"A camera? What the fuck is a camera doing out here? Who are you?"

Jodi and Ilima and Trent laugh and run off, but Duncan keeps digging through the man's recycling bin.

"I'm calling the police." The man disappears back inside his home.

At the top of the next block Victor sets up a shot next to a blue bin, anticipating Duncan's approach. Duncan sprints, and karate kicks the bin right at the top, knocking it over and sending the contents flying. Lights go on in houses on both sides of the street.

"Whoa, Duncan. Cool it," Trent warns.

The next neighbor to come out is an aging jock with a beer belly hanging over his boxer shorts. He is also swinging a baseball bat, which Paul dodges as he feels the rush of air as the bat passes close to his belly. He swings at Victor next, but the Russian war veteran dodges him like an expert, the camera rolling the entire time.

Gasping for air, the jock misses with every swing, which enrages him more. Then he spots Duncan, a much easier target, kneeling on the ground sifting through trash. The jock lifts the bat high and runs at him screaming. Duncan pulls a Heineken bottle from under the BMW in the driveway, then glances up to see the bat coming right at his head.

What happens next seems to be a trick of the eye. Duncan shifts his weight, ducks his head, and as the bat swings past his skull he plucks it out of the jock's hand as easily as if he'd handed it to him. Duncan stands up, shoulders the bat and stares into the man's eyes.

"Please, I won't do anything. Just don't hurt the car," he begs.

Duncan grins, as if the idea just came to him. He swings the bat hard and smashes the back window of the Mercedes, then lifts the garbage bag of recycling onto his shoulder and walks away, leaving the man staring at his damaged automobile.

Trent and Jodi give Duncan high-fives, but Ilima is still scared.

"We always get hassled when we do this."

"Fuck them, this is just trash to them. We need the money," Trent says.

Ilima goes into another coughing fit, as much from fear as sickness. Her face turns ashen and then she vomits up all her beer and pancakes. The others skip away from the mess, laughing and holding their noses. The color returns to Ilima's face and she smiles.

Trent leads them downhill. He glances around, sniffing the air and listening.

"Hide if you hear a car coming. They called the cops for sure."

Duncan nods. The girls come close, aware the boys are nervous. At the first sound of a car engine they all dart down different driveways and crouch behind cars. Victor and Paul join them. A police cruiser drives past, passing Dwight parked but slumped down in the white van.

They get to the recycling center in the supermarket parking lot at 8 a.m. and sell their cans and bottles for nine dollars, then go dumpster diving and find a box of oranges and a red chair missing a cushion. They head back to the subway.

Victor and Paul ride the train with them while Dwight drives the van on the surface streets above. The train is crowded with commuters, but everyone gives the kids room because of their stench, so Victor has plenty of space to sneak his shots.

They get back to the vats by 9:30 a.m. Victor shoots them trudging back upstairs with their new red chair and their oranges, and follows them into their grey cement rooms. Ilima and Duncan go straight to their wooden pallets and Trent and Jodi fall face first onto the dirty mattress they share. They are all unconscious immediately.

A short buzz comes over Victor's ear piece. The Russian takes off his headset and powers down his camera. "That's it for today. They'll be out for at least ten hours."

Paul glances at his watch. He worked fifteen hours without a break.

CHAPTER 11

P aul gets back to Maggie's at 11 a.m. He finds a note on the refrigerator: *So, how was it?* Paul writes in the space provided underneath – *Survived. One day down, forty-one to go.*

He pours himself a huge bowl of cereal and steps in the shower with it. The scalding water pounds the muscles on his shoulders and neck as he munches away.

He is making a thousand dollars a week ... six days a week, that's around a hundred and seventy dollars a day ... he worked fifteen hours a day ... so that is what? Around eleven dollars an hour? Eleven dollars an hour for hard physical labor, most of it at night, working with two guys who didn't like him, chasing after four pitiful losers, and at the end of six weeks he'll have about five thousand dollars after taxes.

Was this even worth it? He could work at McDonald's for six dollars an hour, and he wouldn't be crippling himself, or he could be a temp secretary for some talent agency and make twelve dollars an hour.

But he couldn't do it, he couldn't wear a name tag, or a tie. Not yet. That would be admitting failure. He must be able to tell himself that he is working in his chosen field, even if he's being abused. Then again, this kind of TV work hardly counted as filmmaking. Maybe Maggie made the right choice. At least she has a life.

"Stop it," he says out loud to stop his spinning mind. He shuts off the water. He is a filmmaker working on a production to earn money to get his film made. That's his story, and he is sticking to it.

He steps out of the shower with lobster red skin. Any more poaching and his meat will fall off the bone. But the tension is gone, and he can sleep. He crawls into bed and sets the alarm for 4:30. He'll get five hours of sleep and still have just enough time to eat and rush out the door again.

It is only six weeks, Paul tells himself, and he'll make five thousand dollars. He'll split it three ways – a third will go to catching up on his car payments, a third for credit card debt on his film, and a third to Maggie for back rent and groceries. He will still owe money to all three, but maybe it'll buy him some wiggle room and time.

If he can earn another two thousand he could then transfer the eight minutes of film he shot in the past year to videotape, edit one more scene and smooth out the transitions between two others. A third of his film would be done and enough of a story would be there. He could show it to investors, distributors, and agents. People never give money to start a project, but they love to give money to help finish one. It will all work out. He pulls the comforter up close to him and he smells Maggie's scent on it. He falls asleep.

The alarm seems to go off a moment later.

CHAPTER 12

P aul rides the bus downtown for yet another long night of work. Three weeks have gone by and Paul has found his rhythm. He starts work at 5:30 p.m. and works until sometime between 2 a.m. and dawn, depending on the kids. Then he does maintenance on his gear, stows it in the white van, and takes the bus home.

Half the week he manages to crawl into bed with Maggie for a few hours of sleep before she must get up. The rest of the time he gets home after she's already left for work. On his one day off a week, he sleeps, eats, and washes clothes.

"You're like my golden retriever," she says, scratching his head as he lies on the couch one Sunday afternoon. "I just have to worry about feeding you, that's it."

They've had sex once in three weeks, vanilla sex that felt more like unclogging a drain pipe than making love, and then it was back to work for both of them. The truth is, their relationship is on hold until the six weeks are up, and Maggie seems happy without him. She has her life and her friends, and he is just a warm body that appears and disappears without incident, which seems to suit her just fine.

When he gets off the bus, a silver Lexus is waiting for him. Joel Cuvney steps out. It is never a good sign when the network executive shows up on set (if the vats could be called a set). Either there is a problem that he thinks he can fix, or he is bored and wants to change things, just because he can.

"Paul! How's the job so far?"

"No complaints."

He has a hundred complaints but none that Joel will ever address, so he keeps them to himself. He looks towards the vats and sees that the white van is gone.

"When I showed up Dwight and Victor drove off together somewhere. I think they want to get away from me. We were supposed to have a meeting, but they just drove off." Joel whines like the cool kids don't want to play with him.

"They probably went to get something to eat."

"Did the kids eat pancakes and get high again last night?"

"Yes, they did."

"You know how many hours of tape we have of them sitting in that damn pancake house? What kind of story is that?"

"I'm sure Dwight will be able to edit it down into a good documentary."

"But it's not a documentary!' Joel screams at him. "It's a nonfiction movie! Why can't you people see that?"

"Sorry, nonfiction movie," Paul says.

"This is mundane boring bullshit!" Joel screams, because Paul *is* the audio guy, and low enough in Joel's mind that he feels he can yell at him.

"Ever hear of *Roots*?" Joel yells. "That started as a movie-of-the-week, but they ran it as a mini-series every day of the week for two weeks, and it changed television. That's what we're supposed to be doing, changing television! Instead we're going to end up with two hours of crap."

Paul rocks on his heels, wishing the white van would come back. It's 6 p.m. and the kids must be awake by now.

Joel lights a cigarette, takes a long drag, steps off the curb and stands in front of Paul. He blows smoke. "It really is crap, don't you think?"

It all becomes clear. The producer wants him to say that the director's work is crap. Joel needs an ally against Dwight, and he is offering Paul the job.

"Before I answer that, can I ask you a question, Joel?".

"Go ahead."

"What happened to the last audio guy anyway?'

"He just didn't work out. He was always complaining."

"Complaining about what?"

"Chest pains from overwork. He collapsed one night, and we let him go home early. He went to some doctor who told him he had a heart attack. Now he's trying to sue us, the bastard," Joel says, tossing the cigarette away. "So, what do you say? This is crap, isn't it?"

Paul doesn't know what to do. Normal etiquette says that a crew member never sides against the director; there must be solidarity against anybody in a suit trying to compromise the work. But then again, this is hardly a regular shoot and Dwight and Victor treat him like a doormat. What kind of solidarity is that?

"I haven't been here the whole shoot, but I'm having trouble following the story."

"Exactly!" Joel yells, dancing on his feet. "Dwight says that he finds the story once he's in the edit bay, but I don't believe him. We've already shot 500 hours of footage, and it's them eating pancakes night after fucking night!"

Paul has a choice; he can stay an audio guy, and just mention that the sound is good, which is all that matters. Three weeks from now he'll be done, he'll have his five thousand bucks and he'll never have to see these people again. Or, he could cross the line and be *more*. He has opinions, he can tell a story, and when he succeeds there will be plenty of producers like Joel in his future. This could be good practice. He should talk to him and see where it goes.

"The kids have a tough time and their lives are really sad, but their struggle doesn't really fit into a natural story arc with a beginning, middle, and an end. It's the same thing over and over, and nothing is going to change unless these kids get challenged dramatically with a crisis. An inciting incident."

Joel looks at him wide-eyed, as if he had just found his long-lost brother. "That's perfect. You hit it right on the nose."

The white van appears from around the corner and parks in front of the brewery.

"Eyes are on me, I better get to work," Paul says.

He leaves Joel salivating on the curb and walks to the van. Dwight slides out of the driver's seat, slams the door and walks away without even looking at him. Paul opens the back door and reaches for his gear. Victor lies flat on his back on the mattress, boring a hole through the top of the van with unblinking eyes. It's probably his version of sleep, Paul thinks.

As he assembles his gear, he spots Dwight and Joel inside Joel's Lexus, screaming at one another. No sound escapes, but the chassis moves whenever Dwight bangs his fist on the dashboard. Dwight leaves the car and slams that door too, ending the meeting. Joel rolls down his window and yells. "I'm getting everybody dinner! Come on, Paul, I need your help."

Paul freezes and looks at Dwight, who shakes his head *no*.

"I can't, I have to work," Paul says to Joel.

"It's on me! I say it's okay, Dwight. Do you guys want food or not?"

Dwight and Victor stare at Paul, waiting to see what he'll do. Paul looks at his director. "It's your call, Dwight."

Dwight waves his hand with disgust at him, signaling that he can go. Paul shuffles to the car, feeling like a Mafia informer hopping into a police cruiser in front of his gangster buddies. He sinks into the leather seat and Joel spins away.

They go to McDonald's and Joel uses the drive-through and hands the bags to Paul. That's the extent of Paul helping to get dinner, but Joel keeps asking questions.

"So, who's the main character here?"

"Trent is the obvious leader. All the storylines flow from him–"

"That's obvious," Joel interrupts. "I want to know who jumps out at you."

"Duncan has the charisma. He's a loose cannon, but there's something exciting there if you can figure out how to use him."

Joel nods and smiles. Paul feels like he just passed some kind of test.

"Interesting. I'd like to see your film. See what else you're up to."

Joel parks next to the white van. Paul stares straight ahead. "I'll get you a copy," Paul says as he grabs the hamburger bags and gets out. Joel drives away.

"I guess he's not staying for dinner. What did you tell him?" Dwight asks.

"I said you are a mentor, an artist and my inspiration." Paul thrusts his bag of food at him. Dwight glares at him, then smiles. Paul jabbed him with a joke and Dwight had allowed it, which means he is one step closer to being accepted. The three men stand on the curb munching their hamburgers next to the open van.

"I can't believe I'm eating this corporate crap," Dwight mutters. "That cheapskate *would* go to McDonald's." Dwight reaches inside the van and pushes up the sliders on his mixing board and brings up the sound on the hidden microphones inside the vats. Nothing but static. The kids are still sleeping. It's 6:30 p.m. and nothing is happening yet.

Dwight pushes up the volume on the microphones in another room and panting comes out of the speakers. Dwight isolates one microphone as panting becomes groaning.

"That's Jodi," Paul says.

"Sounds like Trent's working that broken middle finger of his," Dwight says.

"He's working more than that," Victor says, and he and Dwight snicker.

It makes Paul hate them even more. Dwight the purist, who insists on remaining detached from his subjects, is laughing at them.

Listening to two homeless kids making love on a filthy mattress is the closest to sex Dwight and Victor were going to get. Paul wants to shout at them that he doesn't need to eavesdrop, he has a real sex life with Maggie – although it's on hold right now, and Maggie doesn't seem to care. Instead, Paul holds his tongue.

Dwight and Victor wolf down the last of their hamburger buns, another meal eaten in five minutes. Dwight lowers the volume for that room and raises up another fader, so he can eavesdrop on Ilima and Duncan.

Duncan and Ilima giggle, then Ilima whispers. "Get away from me! It's so ugly, put it away."

"Duncan has no clue, but he's trying, God bless him." Dwight says. "Let's try to shoot this, we still haven't gotten any decent sex on tape."

Paul doesn't feel like shooting voyeur porn and hopes the kids will finish by the time he and Victor get in there. Paul checks his gear as slowly as he can and clips his audio rig into place across his shoulder and hips. The thick pads on his shoulder harness are still damp from his sweat the night before. Victor grabs his camera and they ease up the creaky fire escape and enter the building without a noise.

Crouching low, they tiptoe between the carpets of broken glass and through the main vat room. Victor hits the "record" button on his camera, then motions for them to creep forward to the kids' living area. Paul holds his boom out, sniffing for sound. They get to the door of the first storage room and Victor eases his camera in, spying…

"Yo!" Duncan screams in their faces and runs away, giggling.

Victor is thrown off balance and almost drops the camera. Ilima stays under her blanket on her pallet, laughing and coughing.

Trent and Jodi walk in, fully dressed. "Let's go get some pancakes!" Trent yells.

Duncan and Ilima dash around pulling the rest of their clothes on and within moments the group tumbles out of the building and heads down the street.

This time the kids end up at Daisy's, an old downtown diner whose sign is a buxom hillbilly girl bursting out of her rag dress. The waitress doesn't mind if they smoke inside, so the kids eat pecan pancakes and ham, then smoke an entire pack of Marlboros between them.

Each one is so different from the other, but this is what they share, Paul thinks. No matter how bad things are, they can always agree on how much they love pancakes and smoking. It isn't much, but it's something.

It makes Paul wonder what keeps Maggie and him together. For a long time, it was sex – they had sex when they were happy, sad, bored, or angry. It was a response to everything. Now that isn't enough for Maggie, she wants something more. She wants a sense of direction and purpose. Paul does too, but he's not sure if he's ready for a big commitment.

Maggie senses this, although he denies it when she asks him. Sex had gradually been replaced by ceaseless talking, especially after he moved in. No matter how much he tells her he is only there until he can pay off the creditors, she still wants to talk about the relationship. That one action – "moving in" – speaks louder than any words he can ever say. As long as Paul isn't honest with himself or her, Maggie will keep her distance. They haven't seen a movie, read the paper in bed, or shared coffee in the morning in weeks. A wave of self-pity hits him … these homeless kids have more true love and affection than he has right now.

Even though he is in debt and working nights as they drift further apart, Paul decides at this moment that he and Maggie must stay together … whatever that means.

Victor elbows Paul – he'd let the boom drift into frame. Paul jerks it up and focuses back on the conversation.

"You get lazy, bastard," Victor hisses at him. Yup, Victor hates him.

The kids argue about whether it's okay to eat the strip around the edge of the ham, or whether you should peel it off. Then they eat all the sugar and NutraSweet out of the packages and argue about which tastes better. They argue about whether to shoplift or to panhandle, and whether to buy beer, speed, weed, or more pancakes. Ilima coughs and spits green phlegm into her paper napkin and shows it to everyone, and they all groan.

Ilima laughs and then is hit with a fit of deep resonant hacking coughs. Her face turns red, then purple as she fights to get control. The waitresses stare at her. Victor gets on his knees and pushes in for a tight shot, framing her face from below. She jumps up from the booth and runs into the bathroom, shutting the door in Victor's face.

The waitress walks up. "You need to get her to a doctor." She puts the bill on the table and stares at them, but Trent and Jodi look down. The waitress walks off.

"We can bring her to the free clinic," Jodi says. "They can give her something."

"Ilima doesn't like doctors," Trent says.

"Maybe we should bring someone to the vats."

No way. The vats stay our secret. If some social worker finds out we're in there, then they'll kick us out or other people will figure out how to get in there with us."

Duncan chews on a paper napkin, wads up a spit wad and shoots it through a straw. It hits the picture of the Hillbilly girl hanging above their booth right on the eye.

"She wants to go to the hospital," Duncan says.

"She does?" Trent asks.

"That's what she says. Except she's not sick enough yet. She wants to get so sick that they let her stay a week, sleeping in a big bed, watching TV and eating Jell-O all day." Duncan shoots another spit wad and it hits the hillbilly girl's other eye. Trent and Jodi look at each other and nod. It's a strategy that makes sense to them.

Ilima returns and sits. She seems okay except her face is ashen.

"You should have your own room. We're going to dig out all the trash from the next storage area down the hall, and that'll be your own space." Trent says.

Ilima beams with their love and acceptance.

"Let's get out of here," Trent says.

Back at the vats the kids clear out the storage space further down the hall. They yank out pieces of pipe and carry them to the main staircase in the vat room and toss them down the stairs, listening to them clang and boom against the cement. They haul out cans of hardened paint and garbage bags full of old paper. In the very back under all the mess they find an old refrigerator with the door missing, with wire racks inside.

"Cool, you've got some shelves," Jodi says.

They drag her pallet down the hallway and position it in the middle of the room, and then bring in the three-legged red chair that they found in Hollywood, along with candles and a flaming mason jar. The room has no trash or bad smells yet, so it looks almost livable.

"There. You have your own room," Jodi declares. "You can sleep all day and all night if you want. No cigarette smoke and no noise. You can get healthy."

Ilima giggles, then coughs deep and rough, like a walrus. "I like it," she says. "But I wish I could really decorate it."

"Let's tag the walls then," Jodi says, and runs into her own room and comes back with a felt tip marker and a can of spray paint, which she hands to Ilima and Trent. She steps over to Paul and pulls two Sharpie markers from his shirt pocket (it happens so fast that Paul has no time to stop her) and hands one to Duncan and keeps the other one for herself. Trent shakes the spray paint can and draws his "tag" repeatedly – a Capital T with the r, e, n, and t twisting out beneath it. Ilima draws her name a dozen times, always dotting the eye with a circle or a happy face. Victor gets a behind-the-shoulder shot as she switches to unicorns, which she draws in large graceful loops. On one unicorn, she draws the horn to look like an erect raging penis.

"This one's named Duncan," she laughs. Duncan just smiles.

Jodi draws the Anarchy symbol then writes a poem:

Sweet like a bird,

Hacks like a Camel,

Ilima has her own room!

Duncan is the slowest. He watches Ilima closely and tries to draw her portrait, but it's not very good; it's closer to a cartoon then an actual likeness.

"I'm no good at this," he complains.

"Don't draw pictures then. Just draw your name," Jodi says.

Duncan throws his pen down and walks out of the room.

"It's okay, it just takes practice," Jodi promises.

Victor gets a shot of Duncan through the doorway, sitting forlorn and self-pitying in the next room, the light playing off his face from the flaming glass jar. Ilima walks into the room and touches his shoulder from behind, comforting him.

A movie moment, Paul thinks. And the lighting is good, too. In fact, the whole evening has been full of moments. The kids are doing something besides eating, stealing, begging and taking drugs. They created a living space for Ilima, drew art on the walls, and expressed concern for one another.

Victor's headset buzzes. He gestures to Paul that they are on break and they retreat to the fire escape. Dwight is waiting for them at the bottom of the staircase with a huge grin on his face.

"Finally! We're in the groove! That's some good scene material!' Dwight says to Victor. Then he turns to Paul and spits. "Except you broke the rules."

"How did I break the rules? I thought we were doing fine in there."

"You gave Jodi two Sharpies to write on the walls."

"I didn't give them to her, she took them," Paul protests. He turns to Victor.

Victor shrugs. "I did not see; my eye was to camera."

"I don't see how it matters that much," Paul says, smiling. "It was Jodi's idea to draw, she already had a felt tip and a spray can. Two more Sharpies, how much difference does that make? Plus, we got some great scene material from it."

"You're not supposed to engage them. It affects the reality of the situation. They could have argued about how to share the two pens, they could have fought, anything could have happened. But you interfered," Dwight says softly, smiling in a patronizing way. "Can you see that now?"

Paul doesn't appreciate the lesson. "We interfere with these people every time we walk into the room with a camera! Did you want me to fight her when she took them?"

Dwight's smile turns to a scowl. He walks back to the van.

I'm blowing it again, Paul thinks. His need to be independent is sometimes too strong, he realizes, and it keeps him from getting what he wants. Big Andy swallowed his pride for years and took orders from stupid people who told him *that they were in charge,* but now Andy oversees his own productions and is moving forward with his career.

But Paul can't tolerate that; he walks out of jobs or barks back at inept bosses whenever he feels he's being treated unfairly, and now he's doing it again and alienating the one guy who can help him get out of debt.

Paul and Victor pee, drink water and eat protein bars. Victor pats him on the back, his first friendly gesture towards him in three weeks of shooting.

"Come on, break's over. We only have few hours to go."

Back inside the loft the kids light more candles and share the last of their marijuana. Ilima puts her hand out to grab the joint as it goes by.

"If you smoke it, you finish it," Jodi says. "I can't afford your germs."

"I need it to sleep tonight. It'll make me feel better."

They try playing a card game but give up because they're too stoned. Trent and Jodi start kissing and petting on the ratty red velvet couch, which makes Duncan and Ilima giggle. Victor starts shooting close-ups of lips and roaming hands, until Trent and Jodi sneak into the next room.

Victor creeps forward and shoots through the doorway as they start making love. He doesn't dare creep any closer; this is the first real sex they have on tape and he doesn't want to risk ruining the moment. Then he moves back into the main room and gets shots of Ilima and Duncan listening to Trent and Jodi moan while pretending to play cards. Duncan reaches over and tries to kiss Ilima.

"I have to go to bed," she says. Duncan watches her go and then moves to the windowsill and plays with one of the lit Mason jars, running his hands in and out of the flames.

Dwight's voice buzzes through Victor's headset. Victor signals that they are done and heads for the fire escape, while Paul pauses for a moment in the main room to power down his gear. Duncan looks up from the flaming Mason jar and catches his eye and smiles. Paul smiles back. Then Duncan points to the back of his head, to the same spot where Paul has his scar, then flashes the thumbs up. Paul then points to his face, to the same spot where Duncan has his scar, and flashes the thumbs up back. Duncan's face lights up with happiness.

CHAPTER 13

Paul catches the last regular bus of the night heading west on Wilshire and gets back to Maggie's at 4 a.m. Sunday morning. Walking up Cochran Avenue at that hour of the morning is soothing. A cool dampness hugs the street and there is no movement in the neighborhood at all. The only noise is the buzzing and clicking from the electronic boxes that turn that streetlights from green to amber to red.

As he approaches Maggie's apartment building, his mind is already slipping between the cool sheets inside her bedroom … and then he spots something that jolts him: the brown Cutlass from the night of the Premiere, with the two repo men fast asleep in the front seat. He pauses for a moment, listening to the big guy's gentle snoring through the open front window.

Paul slides his keys in the lock and pushes the gate open. The iron creaks and both repo men wake up. "Hey! Paul Franti! We need to talk to you!" the smaller one yells.

Paul lets the gate bang shut and gets to Maggie's apartment door. Once inside, Paul peeks out the dark window. The repo men are out on the lawn staring up at the building, trying to figure out the exact apartment where he might be hiding.

How had they figured out that he's living with Maggie? Or where she even lives? These guys are scary serious. Weren't there worse scofflaws driving BMWs and Mercedes they could hassle?

Paul is ticked; he'd been halfway asleep when he got off the bus and now he's wide awake again. He creeps past the open bedroom door and sees Maggie lying there waiting for him, and heads into the bathroom. He pees sitting down, takes a 3-milligram tablet of melatonin, and hears the Cutlass drive away. Then he quietly shuts both the bathroom and bedroom doors and sneaks back into the living room with a half-bottle of red wine and turns on the TV. An old Roger Corman movie from the 1960s is on, *The Man with the X-Ray Vision,* and Paul watches with the sound off until the red wine and the melatonin finally work, and he falls asleep around 5 a.m.

Paul sleeps without moving for five hours straight, and then starts to dream. He is back at work, getting audio as Victor shoots the kids eating huge stacks of pancakes in yet another downtown diner, while Dwight sits three booths away watching on his monitor, whispering instructions into his walkie-talkie. Trent and Jodi break open cigarettes and sprinkle their pancakes with brown tobacco leaves, while Duncan douses his immense stack with cognac brandy and then lights it on fire. Ilima keeps coughing up huge gobs of green and red phlegm that she spits into a side dish.

Paul hears a knocking somewhere. He looks at his gear and spins knobs but can't figure out where the noise is coming from. Victor glances up from his eyepiece and glares – he can hear it too and wants Paul to do something about it. He tries isolating each audio source but that doesn't work, then suddenly Dwight is in front of him, grabbing his boom from his hand –

Paul wakes up. The knocking is coming from the front door. He rolls off the couch but can't stand up because his entire left side is asleep, so he lies on the floor shaking his arm and his leg trying to get the nerves to reconnect. Paul hears the bedroom door open and sees Maggie dart past, pulling a robe around her. He wants to yell out something about the repo men, but he can't speak.

Maggie opens the door. It's some muscular guy with great looks and a perfect tan. "Not now," Maggie whispers. Not now? What does that mean?

He hands Maggie her Sunday paper. "I was just getting mine from in front, and I thought I'd give you yours," he says with a loud British accent. He smiles, then tilts his head and blinks at Paul lying on the floor behind her.

"Thank you, Rupert, that was so sweet of you," she says and turns to Paul writhing on the floor. "Paul! Rupert brought us our morning paper, isn't that nice of him? You remember Rupert, don't you? He lives in the unit above us."

Paul struggles to his feet and limps to the front door as pins and needles sweep through his left side. Rupert comes into focus and Paul recognizes him, although he seems better in much better shape than he was three weeks ago.

"Hello."

"You look horrible, old man. Tough night?"

"More like a tough year."

"Good thing I brought you your paper then. I don't think you'd have made it to the gate and back."

Maggie laughs out loud, and for too long. Paul wonders why his comment is so hilarious and glances at her. Maggie stops.

"Thanks again, Rupert. Good luck with your audition tomorrow."

"Thanks, I'll need it. Nice seeing you again, Paul."

Maggie shuts the door and heads straight to the kitchen and to the coffee maker.

Paul hobbles after her. "He tells you about all his auditions?"

"Sure, you do," she says, filling the filter with French Roast. "He's got a third callback audition for an NBC soap opera tomorrow. He's excited." She hit the red switch.

"He's got a great tan for an Englishman."

"Not all Englishmen are pasty-white. And anyway, he's gay."

"He has a tan because he's gay?"

"I'm saying he's got the whole look going. Perfect hair, tan, the gym body. That's what you do if you're gay," she says while taking the milk out of the refrigerator.

"He sure knocked for a long time."

Maggie pours the milk into two cups. "He's a good neighbor. He's just nervous about his big audition and wants to gossip about it."

"So, you've become friends then?"

"We were friends before you moved in. We check up on each other. And in this neighborhood, it's important to have friends like that. It's not like you're around a lot these days." She pours the coffee, hands him his mug and kisses him. "But I think it's sweet that you're jealous. Even if he is gay."

Why did she whisper *not now* then? He is jealous, he must admit. Had something happened? And just the night before, Paul had decided to commit to Maggie once and for all. He decides not to press either button right now.

They go back into the bedroom and sprawl on the bed to read the paper and sip coffee. The sun shines through the window, music is on the stereo and the pain in Paul's thighs and back gradually fades. After he finishes each section of the *Los Angeles Times* he glances over at Maggie sprawled sideways across a pillow, one leg under the covers and one leg over, her breast just ready to fall out of her loose robe. She senses him looking at her and smiles, tosses her hair and goes back to reading.

"That's not your usual terry cloth robe," Paul says.

"It's silk, I just bought it," she says, running her hand across it. "I got a raise at work, so I decided to treat myself."

"You got a raise? Congratulations."

"Thank you."

"And you look great in it."

"Thank you again.' She smiles.

"Do you want more coffee?" Paul asks.

"Wow, this feels like a first date," Maggie says.

"Maybe it is. Do you want more coffee or not?"

Maggie doesn't answer. She crooks her finger and beckons him. He goes straight for her mouth, and her lips meet him more than halfway and they both push the paper off the bed while still locked in a kiss. He slides his hand into her robe and touches her nipple, and suddenly she is on top of him, her hips across his waist and her white breasts out in the bright sunshine. She laughs and dangles her hair in his face.

"Let's fuck," she says.

And so, they do. And it's wonderful – and different. They've been making love on Sunday morning their entire relationship, so Paul knows what to expect from Maggie's repertoire. But she has new tricks this time around, stuff neither of them ever talked about. She rocks him hard, and his climax drains the last drop of energy out of his body. He passes out for another hour. When he wakes up, Maggie is reading the paper.

"That certainly was different. Where'd you learn all that?"

"Books. I've had lots of time for reading since you took this job."

Paul flashes back to the kids eating their pancakes and smoking, trying to grab at any shared feeling they could, and how badly he wanted a shared feeling too. He'd been waiting for this day with Maggie ever since then, and this Sunday morning was turning out perfect, exactly how he'd hoped. In just a few hours she'd restored him and prepared him for another 90-hour week.

"Maggie."

"Yeah?"

"You know how you asked me if I was living here or hiding here? And I said both? Well now I feel like I just want to live here. With you. For a very long time."

Maggie's face softens, and she kisses him. "That's so sweet."

She rolls to the edge of the bed and stands up. "But you're so busy with your job right though, that I think you were right when you said we should wait and see. Until after the six weeks is up, I mean."

Paul feels like the bed has disappeared from under him, and he is in freefall.

She grabs his mug and holds it up with a smile. "More coffee?"

When Paul wakes up Monday morning, Maggie is dressing for work.

"Hey Sleepyhead. You almost missed your show." She turns to face him, zipping up her grey skirt alongside her hip.

"You're wearing a skirt. I thought black pant suits are the uniform for you executive types."

"I feel like wearing dresses these days," she says, and buttons her white shirt until it covers up her pink lacy bra.

Maggie seems happy, which makes him happy for her, but also makes him realize how frustrated he still is, and just how little his angst plagues her anymore.

"I'm going to the bank before work today. I can write you a check for half the money I owe you," Paul says.

"What about the money you owe on your car? Shouldn't you pay that first?"

"No. I think it's more important to pay you back."

"Okay. Thank you very much." She picks up her purse and her keys. "Another late night tonight?"

"Yeah, but only two more weeks and it's done.'

"Don't worry, they'll fly by." She leans over the bed and kisses him fast, then is out the door.

Paul tries to sleep but he can't stop thinking about his bills, his film, then the English actor Rupert, and then Dwight, and Joel, and then his bills again.

He finally jumps in the shower to stop his mental spin cycle.

He considers driving his car to the bank, but when he steps outside the repo men are already parked and waiting for him in their brown Cutlass. The smaller guy smiles and waves from the front seat.

"The dealership would still like to have its car back, Mr. Franti."

"I'm going to put money in the bank right now."

"They don't want your money anymore. They want their car."

"We see each other a lot. What's your name anyway?"

The repo man laughs. "You want to know my name? Fuck you, you deadbeat loser. I'll tell you my name when you tell me where you're hiding that car."

Paul walks down the street, and the brown Cutlass follows him. He rides the bus to the bank, he deposits his checks and buys toothpaste and shampoo, and the brown Cutlass trails him the whole time. They even follow him back to Maggie's, slowly keeping pace with him as he walks up the street to her gate.

"All this for a stupid $25,000 Camry!" the small repo man shouts. "You're a loser Franti! Fuck you!" and the Cutlass speeds away.

It's 3 p.m. Paul sits at the computer and stares at page fourteen of his screenplay about the genetically-engineered super kids for an hour until it's time for work. He'd just enjoyed thirty-six hours off, the most time since he started the project. He grabs his jacket, locks the apartment, goes out the front gate – and spots Joel Cuvney parked in his silver Lexus.

"You want a ride to work?"

Paul hesitates.

"Come on, don't tell me you'd rather ride the bus," he laughs.

Dwight won't be happy if he takes the ride. But how much loyalty does he feel for Dwight and Victor anyway? During the last four weeks of shooting there has been zero camaraderie, mostly because there is no downtime to even chat and get to know one another. They were either working, peeing, eating, drinking, commuting or sleeping. In six weeks, he'd spoken less than an hour total to Dwight and Victor combined. Paul could probably get to know Dwight better if he tried harder, but Dwight isn't trying either. And here is Joel at Maggie's front door, making the effort to meet him.

Paul sinks down into the plush leather seats. German electronic music is on the stereo, and within moments they are on the Santa Monica Freeway headed east towards downtown, back to the poor homeless kids in their abandoned brewery.

"Give it to me straight. Do we have a story yet?"

"I don't know. It depends on what happens in the edit bay," Paul says.

Joel nods behind his sunglasses. "That's still the big question. We have two more weeks of shooting and I don't even know what kind of story I'm producing."

"We've been getting some amazing stuff though," Paul says.

"Hey, no doubt, I watch the footage and some of it is dynamite. On Friday, the whole office was looking at Duncan parading around with his hand on fire. That was wild. But if I have to watch another tape of them eating those fucking pancakes I'll burn down the fucking restaurant myself, with them inside. Then at least we'll have an ending."

They drive a minute in silence, curving off the 10 Freeway to the 110, and down the 4th Street downtown exit.

"I finally saw that short film you did. It's quite good."

"I gave you that a while ago," Paul says.

"Hey, I got to it, didn't I?" Joel laughs. "Accept the compliment. I'm telling you that you know how to tell a story. At least as good as that asshole Dwight."

A tingle shoots up Paul's spine. Joel is laying groundwork for a plan, probably a plan that involves him betraying Dwight. They go through downtown, cross Alameda Boulevard and pass the endless rows of cardboard boxes where the homeless street people live. Paul sinks low in his seat, suddenly scared that Dwight is somewhere close by and watching them.

"What would you do different with these kids?"

"It's a documentary. We're just supposed to be following them."

"I know that," Joel says, suddenly impatient. "But it's also a made-for-TV movie. You said they need to have a crisis that challenges them. How would you do that?"

They are getting close to brewery. Paul can see the white van in the far distance and imagines Dwight spotting them even from there.

"You can let me off here. I'll walk the last three blocks," Paul says.

Joel pulls over. Paul tries to open the door, but it's locked. He looks over at Joel, who smiles. He pulls out an envelope and hands it to him.

"There's two thousand dollars in there."

"What for?"

"That's your story consulting fee for the advice you've been giving me."

Paul quickly calculates – two thousand is half of what he still owes Maggie, a quarter of what he owes in car payments and a fifth of what he owes the film lab. He folds the envelope and sticks it deep in the front pocket of his jeans.

"Thanks," Paul says, and the car door magically unlocks.

Joel grabs his arm. "I need an ending. Do what you can to make something happen, Paul. Please. We don't have much time left."

CHAPTER 15

Trent keeps the tribe moving and gets them money, and is therefore the father. Jodi decides how the money is spent and with whom the tribe can hang, and is therefore the mother. When she isn't dancing, or preening, Ilima whines and pleads for everything, which makes her the daughter. Duncan, on the other hand, is just *there*.

The truth is, Ilima doesn't need to have a dog with Duncan around. He is their dog. He is always present and usually does very little, until something sets him off. He might hear or smell something none of the others sense yet, or lash out at anyone threatening them. Like when three street punks tried to corner Ilima in a club in Hollywood and Duncan body-slammed one against the wall and kept kicking him until Trent and the other two punks pulled him off.

Or like a dog, he'll spontaneously do something in public that is both hilarious and completely inappropriate, like standing up in the pancake house and directly farting at two police officers in the next booth. Or he will shamelessly grab his stiff penis in his pants whenever something arouses him, until Ilima or Jodi slap him and tell him to stop.

It's coming close to the end of shooting and Dwight is not happy with what they are getting, so Dwight tells them they will work eighteen-hour days until the end of shooting. Paul accepts his fate. It's Saturday night and he is already doing the countdown: twelve more hours until one day off, and then only five days until shooting ends. Then he can work on salvaging his relationship with Maggie. The two thousand in his front pocket will help.

That night the kids spend all their money – about forty dollars – to go to a late-night punk show deep in the San Fernando Valley. Jodi figures out which bus lines to take and they must leave the vats before sunset to get there on time.

Paul is surprised at how dressed up they get. Jodi re-bleached the roots of her hair with Clorox and water, Ilima bought makeup, and Trent added more rips to his leather jacket. Duncan wears what he always wears.

They board a bus that drives north along a cement section of the L.A. River that hugs Highway 5, then turns left and heads deep into the San Fernando Valley. The Valley is always ten degrees warmer in the summer and the blazing sunset heating the bus windows only makes it worse. The tribe is surrounded by people of all shapes, colors and backgrounds, in suits or in t-shirts, people all too exhausted from the heat to even give them a second look. The whole bus smells like tangy human sweat mixed with diesel fuel. Trent, Jodi and Ilima are dressed in vinyl and black leather, which must be torture to wear in the summer heat. They look miserable. Ilima's cheap makeup is already dripping.

Outside through the window Paul can see Dwight racing alongside the bus in the white panel van, insane and driven.

They get to the club after a two-hour bus ride. It's an old boxing arena that the owners haven't fixed in years, which makes it perfect for punk shows. Every week the kids trash the place, and each week new graffiti, blood and puke stains made the place that much more authentic.

It seems odd to be so deep in the suburbs and to see so many punkers, but Paul understands the anachronism, having dabbled in punk himself back home in middle-class Andover. Punk thrives in the suburbs, where every kid must shout to be heard over the mind-numbing hum of avocado-colored refrigerators. And these kids are suburban punks. Their clothes are clean, and the holes in their pants and jackets have been added strictly for effect. They don't stink, they have no oozing open sores, and none of them have a hacking smoker's cough or serious bronchitis.

So, when Trent and his tribe walk up to the door, the crowd of suburban punks parts to let them pass. Trent and the tribe aren't wanna-bes; they are real gutter punks who squat downtown with the drug addicts and the homeless people. Having the camera crew there adds yet another layer of adoration, and for Trent and Jodi the hassle of the two-hour bus ride is worth it. Their tribe is royalty here, and they love it.

Paul swings his boom around and catches the whispers.

"I've seen them before ... he's the head guy ... he's from New York ... I think that's his band..."

The crowd may love them, but the two USC football players who are the bouncers at the front door don't care about the kids at all. They are big fullbacks with USC sweatshirts, one is black and the other white, and they both still have baby fat and pimples around their necks.

The bouncers pat the kids down and wave them into the club. When Victor and Paul try to get in, however, the bouncers insist on examining Victor's camera and Paul's audio rig. Victor refuses to hand over his camera, so the bouncers block them at the door. They let Dwight in, however, who promises to solve the issue.

"I'll go find the owner. You guys just chill."

Victor and Paul step aside to wait, but the bouncers keep bothering Victor. This is the one time when Paul is glad that cameramen get all the attention.

"You got a gun in that thing? A knife?" the white bouncer asks.

"The whole thing might be a bomb," the black bouncer says.

"You're not police," Victor says.

"What did you say?" the black bouncer asks.

"I used to shoot the show *Cops,* and you are not police, so quit trying to act like police. You are college boys who like to bother with people."

"What kind of accent is that?" the white bouncer asks. "Italian?"

When the bouncers ask a third time and Victor refuses to answer, the white bouncer reaches for the camera. Victor grabs the guy's thumb and breaks it.

The fullback falls to his knees, howling. When his pal moves forward, the Russian jabs him in the Adam's apple, and he falls to his knees too. The crowd cheers.

Then the club owner, a small Persian man in a blue suit, comes out with his son and they are both carrying guns. They don't wave them around, they just hold them in their hands, but that is enough to quiet the crowd. Everyone backs away, leaving a wide semi-circle. They kick the two bouncers out of the doorway, then banish Dwight and Victor to the street. The son now examines IDs and takes money, while the owner waves his gun at whoever he thinks should be let in.

Dwight and Victor sit on the curb and Paul walks over to join them. He tests his radio mics, trying to pick up any noise.

"Who's wearing a microphone?" Dwight asks

"Trent and Jodi, but I'm not getting anything."

"Did you put in fresh batteries?" Dwight says this in an accusing way.

"Yes, but they may have knocked them, or they're sweating so much that it shorted the unit out."

Dwight exhales sharply through his nose. Not good enough.

Paul stares up at the marquee, which lists three punk bands in black letters against a white background: *The Stabbers, Murder Boys, and The Racing Stripes*. In his mind, he tries to rearrange the letters into his name and the name of his movie, but it doesn't quite work.

"Which TV station is this going to be on?"

Paul looks down. Three healthy teenage girls stand in front of them, suburban punks with smooth round skin, all of them pretty, even with their "Friar Tuck" bowl haircuts. They are all in sleeveless t-shirts, with thick cotton shirts tied around their waists, ripped black jeans and Doc Marten boots.

"We're doing a documentary on four kids who are inside the club right now, but we couldn't get in," Dwight answers.

"You want to film me instead?" the second girl asks Paul.

"No thanks, not right now." Dwight smiles at them.

The third girl flips them off and they walk away, ending all chance at conversation. Paul shakes his head and Dwight spots it.

"What? You don't like how I handled that, Mr. Franti?"

"We're going to be stuck out here for another three hours and they wanted to talk. What's the harm in talking to them?"

"Talking to them is not part of your job."

Paul grabs his gear and heads down the street.

"Where do you think you're going?"

"To that donut shop there, to get some coffee and read the paper."

"Get your ass back here, they'll be out soon."

"They won't be coming out for hours. And if they do, you can fire me."

Paul turns and keeps walking. His legs are shaking, and he is suddenly wide awake. He did it. He stood up to Dwight and the world didn't cave in.

In the donut shop he orders hot chocolate – he doesn't need coffee; his mind is too buzzed all ready. No donuts, though. Over the weeks, he'd grown to cherish the hollow hungry feeling in his stomach. At first, he filled that hollowness with junk food and gained five pounds in the first week, all in his gut. So, he stopped eating and kept to coffee. Stay mean and lean, that's the way to deal with exhaustion.

He sips his drink and tries to read the paper, but he just stares at the same paragraph. He glances out the window and can see Dwight and Victor fifty feet away sitting on the curb with their heads together, then glancing back at him.

They're talking about me. Good. Some part of him wishes that Dwight would fire him. It would give him an excuse to call Dwight's bluff, because at this point there is no way they could find another audio man and package willing to put up with this kind of abuse.

Paul glances outside again. Dwight is now yelling at Victor, who gets up from the curb and yells back. That's new. The dictator is yelling at his most trusted solider, which is a mistake. Victor is loyal, first and foremost.

Paul drinks too fast and burns his tongue. Shit. The burn is bad enough that he'll taste sandpaper for three or four days.

"You got any ice water?" he asks the Asian grandmother behind the counter.

She points at her tongue and smiles. She'd seen this happen before. She fills up a big cup with icy slush.

"Cup and ice cost twenty-five cents," she says.

Paul hands over a quarter and sips, letting the ice rest on his tongue. This happens on every production. People push each other too far and then overreact to inane stupid shit. And Dwight isn't worth it. Just a few weeks ago, he'd known this man only by reputation – a rebel outsider who crafted singular films of independent vision. Now Paul knows that he accomplished that by being a self-centered prick. Let him do his weird movies; if you are smart, you learn not to work with him.

"You a punk?" the grandma asks.

"I'm just following some of them. For a TV show."

"They'll be out soon. That's why we stay open. Good money on show nights."

"How soon before they let out?"

She glances at the clock on the wall. It's 2:00 a.m.

"They'll be out at 2:15. It's always the same. We got all the donuts ready."

Paul lets the ice roll across his burnt tongue and hefts up his gear again. Time to end his fluorescent *Nighthawks* moments and get back to work.

"Would you mind if we shot in here when the kids get out? For TV?"

The grandma shrugs and nods. "Sure."

Dwight and Victor are back sitting on the curb when Paul walks up.

"You done blowing off steam?" Dwight asks.

"I came back because they'll be out in five minutes."

"How do you figure that?"

"I keep my ears open."

Dwight snickers and Victor joins in. Dwight doesn't move, so neither does Victor. But Paul notices that Victor did glance at his watch to check the time. Paul powers up his rig and clicks it back into place on his harness.

It is now 2:15, and there is no noise from the club except for the distant throb of the same three-note song. Maybe the grandmother is wrong.

Then it happens. The doors burst open and the whole club spills out into the streets at once, with punks leaping over each other like it's a prison break. Paul points his boom and can hear Mozart wafting through the club's speakers and out the door, pushing the kids out as if it's a bad smell.

Victor and Dwight scramble to get their gear working in the middle of a river of screaming kids flowing past them.

"Where are they?" Dwight shouts.

Paul spots Jodi talking with a huge black kid dressed in torn plaid. He pushes her up against a wall, searching for a kiss. Paul waves at Dwight and Victor.

"Jodi, one o'clock. I need to check her mic!"

"Ilima and Duncan behind us! Headed to the donut shop!" Victor shouts, and he takes off with his camera towards the donut shop while Paul runs to corner Jodi.

Paul hugs his gear close to him as he maneuvers through the crowd. Kids scream and whack at his boom pole, sending thumping shock waves through his headphones. He reaches Jodi and her new friend and coughs to let them know he's there. When the guy turns, Paul freezes – he has a huge safety pin through his upper lip.

"I need to check your transmitter."

"It works fine, I just turned it off. I didn't want you spying on me."

"Would you mind turning it back on?"

"She'll turn it on when she's ready, asshole." The guy steps forward, chest out. She grabs his shirtfront.

"It's okay, Xander, he's one of the cool ones," Jodi says. She snaps her transmitter back on. "Go ahead, Paul. Spy away."

"Just doing my job." Paul steps back and tunes her audio into his headphones.

"Nice weather we're having wouldn't you say?" Jodi says.

"Certainly, lovely weather," Xander laughs.

Paul then hears a sigh through his headphones – Trent is back on-line somehow, but his signal is crackling. Paul spins around and spots him on the curb a hundred yards away, staring at Jodi and his new rival.

Paul crosses the street. Trent looks up at him, pain in his eyes.

"Mind if I check your battery?"

"Just give me a fresh one, I know how to switch it," Trent says. He lifts his shirt, turns off the transmitter and pops out the nine-volt battery. Paul hands him a new one along with a small cloth from his kit.

"You're sweating salt, just wipe everything off," Paul says.

Trent wipes everything carefully while watching Jodi and Xander across the street.

"They're just talking about the weather," Paul offers

"Yeah right. She already invited him back to see the vats."

"That doesn't mean they're going to get married."

"She still might fuck him. And then he'll know where we live."

The tone in Trent's voice reveals that Xander knowing where they live is the most serious threat.

"I'm sure Dwight will help you guys figure something out."

"Bullshit. Getting overrun by squatters and kicked out of the place would be a great story. You guys would love that."

"You could always kick us out."

"It's too late for that now."

Paul spots Dwight a hundred yards away, staring at him. He points at his headphones then wags his finger at Paul – he'd heard the whole exchange. Dwight points at the donut shop.

"Sorry, I have to go."

"Yeah, right," Trent scoffs. "I'm not interesting enough right now."

Paul leaves Trent on the curb and heads to the donut shot. Dwight intercepts him at the door. "You were talking to Trent!" Dwight yells, right in Paul's face. "And what does Jodi mean, 'he's one of the cool ones?'"

"Do not mess with me, Dwight. I don't need my salary bad enough."

"You're ruining my shoot," Dwight hisses. "You're fucking with my *work.*"

Paul turns down all his microphones, turning Dwight and the world around him into a silent movie. He stares at Dwight's screaming face filling the screen, his yelling barely audible outside his headphones. Paul is most intrigued by a bulging vein shaped like a circle right in the middle of his forehead. Dwight would look good in a close-up.

Dwight's silent screaming face helps Paul see Dwight in a new way. His *work* is where Dwight begins and ends. Anything else – romance, friendships, money, basic human decency – does not exist for Dwight. He sacrifices them all for his *work,* and in exchange he has created a name for himself. Paul wonders what he would do if he were in the same position. He can tell Dwight is almost done yelling and turns up his boom volume again.

"Now, get your ass in there and get a boom on Ilima!"

Paul walks back in the donut shop and blinks to adjust to the harsh fluorescent light. Every plastic booth is packed with fresh-faced kids wolfing down donuts.

Ilima and Duncan are in the middle booth holding court, surrounded by adoring punk wanna-bes impressed by their whole smelly downtown deal, plus there is a camera shooting it all. Victor stands on a table, framing his shot from above. Paul walks over and sticks his boom pole into position.

A freckled face girl in $500 black leather pants leans in to Duncan, who munches on an apple fritter. "Can I have kiss?"

"If you buy me a dozen donuts," he gulps.

Paul can't help thinking the kid should ask for more than just donuts – like fifty bucks for real food, medicine for Ilima, or new clothes – but Duncan doesn't think that way. The girl kisses him with an open mouth, wipes away the food remnants, then goes up to the counter. Victor's headset buzzes with direction from Dwight. He swings around for the reaction shot from Ilima. Right on cue, she looks jealous. Duncan stares at her with his mouth full.

"What?"

Ilima coughs. The profound hacking goes on for three minutes, deep and resonant, like a calling animal. The place falls silent as the crowd at her table leans away. She grabs a napkin and spits up another thick wad of green and red phlegm. The girls at the table grimace. One guy, a skinny Mexican-American punk in soiled jeans and a t-shirt smiles at her.

"That's so cool," he says.

Ilima smiles back at him. The girl returns with more donuts and Duncan keeps eating. Victor jumps off the table and gets low for the wide shot.

Paul changes position and glances at his watch. It is 3 a.m. Almost quitting time. Almost the weekend, almost his day off, almost time with Maggie again…if these kids would just hurry up.

The door swings open and Jodi steps inside. She nods at Duncan and Ilima.

"We got a ride with Xander, you guys. Let's go."

Duncan and Ilima hesitate.

"If you don't come now, you ride the bus back," she says, and leaves.

Duncan grabs his dozen donuts, looks at his freckle-faced fan in the leather pants and nods at her to come along. Not to be outdone, Ilima grabs the skinny Mexican-American punk by the shirt sleeve and drags him out too.

"See you next Saturday," Grandma says. "Bring your friends!"

Xander is behind the wheel of a rusty beat-up Lincoln Continental, Trent is in the backseat sulking, while Jodi stands in the open passenger door, gesturing for everyone to hurry up.

"Who the hell are these people?" Jodi asks, pointing at Ilima and Duncan's new friends, not even looking at them.

"I'm Shari," the leather girl says.

"I'm Carlton," the Mexican-American kid says.

"It's not cool to show them the vats," Jodi says.

"What about the guy driving? You're showing him." Ilima says.

"Seven people can't fit in the car," Jodi says.

"Eight," announces Dwight, who pulls up in the van. "Victor's riding too."

"I've had ten people in here!" Xander shouts from the driver's seat. "Get in!"

That's all they need. Ilima, Duncan, Shari and Carlton pile into the back seat, crushing Trent while Jodi climbs in the front, squeezing in close to Xander. Victor gets in the front too, rolling down the passenger window and gesturing for Paul to shut the door. Paul pushes the door against Dwight's back until he hears the door click. The camera is on Victor's shoulder, but half of it sticks out into open air. Xander revs the engine.

"Lock that door!" Dwight yells.

Paul flicks the switch on Victor's camera, so the audio will come through his camera microphone, then slaps down the passenger door lock just as Xander squeals away from the curb.

Dwight drives up in the white panel van. Paul jumps in the passenger seat and Dwight takes off after them, pushing it to fifty miles an hour just to catch up.

Mounted on the ceiling of the van right next to Dwight's head is a small monitor that receives the microwave broadcast from Victor's camera, and Dwight glances at it as he weaves through traffic. Paul pushes up the volume on Trent and Jodi's radio microphones, and he can hear Xander making "beep beep" noises like the Roadrunner cartoon. Jodi laughs hysterically.

"Are you hearing this?" Paul asks. "Xander's a piece of work."

"Then you should have put a radio microphone on him," Dwight says.

"I didn't have time. That's why I turned on the camera microphone. It's three feet away, pointed right at him."

Dwight glances up and stares at the monitor while still going fifty, then takes one hand off the wheel to press his walkie-talkie.

"Pan to the back, I want to see Trent's reaction," he barks at Victor, his eyes never straying from the monitor. They're coming up fast on the rear end of a Toyota Tercel.

"Dwight," Paul says, but there is no reaction. "Dwight? Dwight!" The director sees the car ten yards before impact, swerves across the yellow line into oncoming traffic, dodges a honking Volkswagen, passes the Tercel and gets back in his lane. He looks back at the monitor and hits the walkie-talkie.

"More reaction shots of the new kids – damn!" The monitor goes fuzzy. "They're out of transmitter range." Dwight turns off the monitor and looks around. "If we take Vineland, we can beat them there," Dwight says and makes a left turn.

Dwight grips the wheel with white knuckles. Paul turns off his rig to save battery power and tries to breathe slowly, and then feels a strange wave of emotion run through him. He admires, despises and fears Dwight, all at the same time.

He admires his focused intensity and absolute refusal to accept anything that isn't done his way. He despises Dwight for not acknowledging anyone else's thoughts, feelings, contributions, or the existence of anyone who isn't directly helping him with his project. But most of all he feels fear – but not fear of Dwight. He is afraid for himself, because he is more like Dwight than he likes to admit.

Paul already knows he is self-absorbed; Maggie reminds him of that all the time. The world is just a backdrop for the film Paul is constantly creating in his own mind, and she makes Paul feel guilty about it. It keeps him separate from the world. Separate from her.

But Dwight feels no guilt for his behavior at all. Nothing matters except the documentary he is creating, and he will run over anyone to get what he wants. And Dwight is only directing a documentary TV movie with a three-man crew and a cast of four. He is semi-successful at best. What kind of madness is required to direct a feature film? Must he become even more like Dwight? Surpass him in self-obsession to succeed?

Dwight stops at a red light. It is three in the morning and there is no traffic for miles in either direction, so Paul expects Dwight to run the red. But he doesn't. They sit staring at the red shiny disc. It's so quiet that Paul can hear the electric buzz of the streetlights through the window.

"What do you and Joel talk about?" Dwight asks.

"Joel who?"

"Very funny. The guy who gives you rides in his shiny silver Lexus, you smartass."

"We talked about you, what do you think?"

"That's fucked up. You don't work for that suit. You work for me."

"He's paying my salary. And you never offered me a ride once in six weeks."

The light turns green and Dwight takes off, laying the accelerator to the floor.

"You're plotting against me, is that it?"

"Don't worry. I lie through my teeth and tell him you're a joy to work with."

Dwight extends his middle finger and makes mad stabbing gestures, as if his digit was a knife and he could kill Paul with it.

"Relax, Dwight. I'm not a snitch. Joel's afraid you're going to take the footage and do whatever you want with it, and ignore him. And I tell him that he's right, that you probably are."

"You got that right. And if you mess with me, I'll fire you."

Dwight's short cut works. When they reach the corner where Lankershim, Vineland and Camarillo intersect, Paul looks right and sees the Lincoln coming down Lankershim swerving back and forth across the empty lanes of traffic. He powers his kit back up again and puts on his headphones. Jodi is still laughing, but Trent screams in the back seat.

"Don't do it, don't do it!" comes blaring through Paul's headphones.

The Lincoln swerves across two lanes and runs the red light, right in front of their panel van. Dwight gives the street a quick glance and follows. He clicks his monitor back on and gets Victor's shot on screen.

"Victor, I'm back. Pan around, show me what's up."

Victor zooms in on Jodi laughing as Xander yanks the wheel back and forth. He pans into the back seat and shows Trent pounding his fist into the ceiling in frustration. Ilima is passed out against Duncan, completely gone, while Duncan, as usual, is bothered by nothing and just eats donuts. The two new kids are frozen in open-mouth horror.

Paul adjusts the microphones and looks up, and sees Xander swerve from the far-left lane to the far right and up onto a freeway on ramp.

"Bastard kid, we almost lost the camera!" Dwight screams.

"Then quit chasing him, he's just doing it to outrun us!" Paul screams back.

"I have to chase him, this is the best stuff we've gotten in days," Dwight says, and he yanks the car onto two wheels and races up the on ramp after them.

They are on Highway 101 speeding towards downtown. Traffic is light, mostly big delivery trucks that came over the hill into pre-dawn Los Angeles from the Central Valley. Xander swerves between the trucks, doing his best to torment Dwight.

Jodi screams. "This is it, this is the exit! This is it!"

Xander swerves into the exit lane and bounces off the side barrier and the front passenger door pops open. The camera flies off Victor's shoulder and bounces across the asphalt, shooting sparks like a tossed cigarette. Dwight sweeps into the exit lane right behind the Lincoln, and a metal piece of the broken camera bounces up and smashes into the van windshield, shattering it into a spider web. Both men scream.

White noise gushes out of Paul's headphones. He turns everything down as Dwight slams on the brakes to avoid smashing into the Lincoln, which coasts down the off ramp with its passenger door wide open and Victor's butt hanging an inch above the moving asphalt. Duncan, from the back seat, somehow leaped over the front seat and grabbed Victor's belt before the cameraman hit the ground. Victor hangs onto Duncan's arm and two men pull hard to keep Victor from dying.

"We've got to get that camera," Dwight says, as if somehow it still existed.

"They'll stop down here, they have to," Paul says.

But Xander doesn't stop. He runs the stop sign at the bottom and makes a left under the freeway. Dwight pulls the van off to the side and watches the car tear down Silverlake Boulevard, with Victor still hanging out in open space.

"We're fucked!" Dwight screams.

It takes ten minutes to find all the camera remains. The battery is intact, but the rest of the camera is destroyed. The lens was run over, the electronic guts were smashed, but the videotape is still good.

"Whatever is the last thing on this tape is one expensive shot," Paul says.

"You little prick. You didn't lock the door."

"Yes, I did. It popped open when they hit the guard rail."

"I told you to do it!"

"Maybe he shouldn't have gotten into the car in the first place!"

When they get back to the vats, Victor is standing outside on the curb next to the Lincoln. His face is ashen. Laughter drifts down from the upstairs windows.

"They're up there with a case of beer that Xander had in his trunk. They're celebrating putting one over on us."

"You okay?" Dwight asks.

Victor shakes his head. "No. I was almost reality roadkill."

"You okay to work?" Dwight asks.

"How? Camera is gone."

"We have the small digital camera. We can hook up a microphone to the top and still get quality audio."

Victor laughs. Dwight just succeeded in amazing even him.

"When will we get a real camera?" Victor asks.

"Tomorrow, if Joel insured the camera like I told him to. Until then, we're shooting."

"How can you direct? There's no transmitter to the monitor," Victor asks.

"I'll go in and watch what you're doing. Hollywood old-school style."

It takes five minutes for Paul to rig a small microphone to the top of a handheld digital video camera, and Victor is ready to go. Because there is no way to transmit video to the van, Dwight must go in with him to see what is happening.

Victor grabs the hanging rope and pulls the fire escape down into place. Victor heads up the stairs, with Dwight right behind him. When Paul tries to follow, Dwight stops him.

"Victor's got the audio now, you're not needed."

"If something happens with the audio, are you going to fix it?"

"Fuck it. You can come in, but just listen. Stay out of my way."

There had always been two men on the fire escape at most, never three, and as they walk up the stairs another bolt pops out. The whole structure shudders and falls another two inches under their weight. They dart up the rest of the metal stairs and dash through the window.

"I won't use that again," Victor says. "I already almost died once tonight.'

All the fire pots are going in the main room when Victor, Dwight and Paul walk in.

"Hollywood's back! Don't you guys ever give up?" Jodi says. Everyone else in the room laughs.

Victor tracks the length of the room, establishing where everyone is sitting. Speed metal blasts from a small portable boom box that Xander brought, and he dances wildly in the middle of the room. Jodi dances with him, trying to match his frenzy. Trent sits on one of the pallets, staring at the twirling Xander with boredom and hatred, while Shari and Carlton sit on an opposite pallet sipping beer and watching with wide-eyed wonder as the freak show unfolds.

Paul sneaks away from the group and creeps down the hallway alone. Ilima is in her new bedroom, passed out face down on her bed. Duncan sits beside her.

"Her breathing sounds real funny," Duncan says.

"We'll do something about it as soon as we can," Paul says.

A crashing noise comes from the other room – Paul darts back in time to see Xander picking himself up off the floor. He'd spun himself and crashed onto a pallet. Jodi falls onto the couch, laughing, and Victor moves in for a close shot.

Still laughing, Xander crawls along the floor and ends up at the couch between Jodi's legs. She touches his cheek. He smiles and buries his face between her legs. Xander reaches up and grabs her jeans by the belt loops and starts to pull her pants down.

Fear hardens her face. "Cool it. Not right now."

Xander sticks out his tongue and waves it at her, showing off a huge bolt through the center of it. "You don't know what you're missing."

When he tugs harder on her jeans Jodi slaps him, and he bites her on the arm. The punk persona falls away fast, and Jodi looks like a scared high school kid again.

"Get out of here, asshole! Leave!" Jodi screams.

Trent grabs Xander by the back of the jacket and yanks him back on his ass.

"You heard her! Get out!"

Xander, despite being drunk, scissor-kicks Trent and knocks him down to the ground. Unlike Trent and Duncan's faux fighting on Hollywood Boulevard, this violence is real. Xander is larger and stronger and instantly overpowers Trent, punching him in the chest, then head-butting his skull against the cement floor. Trent is out cold.

Xander stands up and smiles at Jodi. "You like my beer, but you don't like me?" He grabs her wrist and pulls her off the couch. "You liked me fine an hour ago. Or was that just to make your boyfriend jealous?" Xander twists her wrist until Jodi falls to her knees in front of him.

"Do something," Shari whispers to Carlton, who shakes his head.

"Get the fuck out of here!" Xander yells, and Carlton and Shari run from the room. Xander doesn't yell at Victor or Dwight, however. He looks at the camera and smiles. "Let's see you put this on TV," he says, and brings Jodi's face close to his crotch.

Paul glances at Dwight and Victor, waiting for the director to tell the cameraman to stop. There are three of them, together they can stop whatever is happening. But Dwight motions for Victor to keep rolling.

Paul realizes then that he can never be like Dwight. He wants to stop it – they still have time to stop it – but he can't do it alone. Xander is stronger than he is, and Dwight and Victor won't help him.

Duncan's whistling starts in the hallway. He strolls into the room with his hands in his pockets. Victor steps back and gets a panning shot that starts on Duncan's face in the doorway, then moves across the room and comes to rest on Xander standing in the middle of the room with Jodi at his feet.

"Leave!"

Duncan doesn't move.

"All of you! You too, cameraman! Get out!" Xander screams.

Jodi weeps, all her tough veneer now gone. She looks back at Victor and Dwight, whom she's ignored or flipped off for weeks. No help is coming from them. She looks over at Paul and makes eye contact. "Please, Paul. Please..."

"Fuck you guys! You want to see me break her neck? For your TV show?" Xander yanks Jodi's hair. He then turns and kicks Trent in the ribs, waking him up.

Paul looks at Duncan, standing five feet away from this screaming angry violent man. Paul nods to do something, and Duncan smiles back. Duncan isn't scared, and he doesn't look at Xander as much as scan him, his eyes darting back and forth, taking in every detail.

"Fine! You guys can watch! Unzip me, bitch! Get to work!" Jodi unzips his trousers, her hands trembling. Xander helps her by yanking his pants down over his butt cheeks, and his erect penis springs forth, hitting Jodi in the nose. She sobs, but no noise comes out.

That's when Duncan moves. He hits Xander full force in the chest with his whole body and knocks him six feet through the air and onto the cement. Xander tries to gasp, but there is no wind left in his lungs.

Jodi runs to Trent. They grab each other and run from the room.

Xander struggles to get his pants up when Duncan sweeps up one of the hot flaming Mason jars with his bare hands and throws the flaming liquid contents right at Xander's crotch. Xander screams as his pubic hair and cotton cargo pants light up. He howls, rolling back and forth across the cement floor trying to extinguish the flames. Duncan then smashes him in the back of the head with the empty glass Mason jar. He doesn't feel it; the growing fire in his crotch possesses him. He struggles to his feet with his pants near his knees and hop-runs down the hallway towards the fire escape. Dwight, Victor, and Paul run after him.

Xander tumbles onto the fire escape, and the final bolt breaks loose. Paul, Dwight and Victor watch from the open window as the entire four-story fire escape sheers away from the brewery in front of them, falling into the empty street with a bare-assed Xander still riding it. He leaps clear just before the metal structure smashes to Earth, but both he and the two tons of metal bounce hard off the asphalt in an ear-splitting crash. They can hear Xander grunting over the din of bending steel, and he rolls to a stop by the padlocked metal front door, unconscious. The door opens and Duncan steps outside, carrying a six pack of beer and an old blanket. He opens the beer cans one-by-one and pours them on Xander's still smoldering crotch and pants until the fire is out. He then tosses the dirty blanket over his nakedness.

Duncan stands up tall, turns his face towards the camera, then looks out the skyline with his chin up. Paul can't help thinking what a great shot it is.

CHAPTER 16

A day later, Paul gets a call that a second camera is ready, and they can resume shooting, but with a call time of noon instead of six p.m. No one mentions the incident with Xander, almost as if it didn't happen. Paul figures Dwight is so anxious to start shooting again that he wants everyone to be working the moment the camera is available, even if the kids are asleep. When he steps outside Maggie's apartment, Joel's Lexus is waiting for him at the curb. He slides into the passenger seat without a word. They drive south on La Brea all the way to the 10 Freeway before Joel even speaks.

"I was able to get another camera."

"Great. So, the insurance came through?"

"Sort of. Almost. It wasn't completely insured. The camera was worth thirty-five thousand and we only insured it for thirty thousand," Joel says.

"That's not bad," Paul says.

"Except there's a lot of paperwork, and we have to rent another camera on top of it. The budget is so damn tight as it is." Joel bites his lip and shakes his head. "And that kid that Duncan almost killed – he has second degree burns across his crotch, a broken wrist, a broken ankle and he needed a dozen stitches across the back of his head. It took ten thousand dollars and a half-day of lawyer's fees to pay him off, and that's after we paid his medical bills. If he'd been anybody important, he could've hurt the project.

"I guess we got lucky," Paul says.

"No, what's really lucky is that we had a strike crew for a TV pilot working ten blocks away at the train station. I sent them over with their Makita drills and crowbars and hammers, and they got that fire escape taken apart and moved to the vacant lot next door within thirty minutes of it falling. The police and firemen never knew what happened."

"Really? They never found out?"

"They better not have. You didn't know? Where were you?"

"Dwight sent me running with his cellphone to find a taxi. I found one in five minutes, directed it back to the vats, and Dwight pushed the kid inside and we rode to the emergency room. Dwight dumped me before we got to the entrance and told me the night was a wrap."

"At least that fucker stopped shooting. Mr. Artist and his Russian hitman had the sense to erase what happened. We still need these last days of shooting."

"Still seems lucky."

We got lucky, but we still lost a lot of money last week. Too much money."

Joel sighs and shakes his head, as if his soul is plagued by regret.

Paul can feel that something else is coming. "What? Say it."

Joel turns off the light music on the stereo and sighs. "We have to cut corners everywhere we can, and Dwight says one way to do that is to let you go a week early."

"What? That would mean today is my last day."

"Exactly. Today is your last day."

"But I have a contract. I signed a deal memo."

"A deal memo is a deal memo, not a contract. And considering what Dwight said I think we're being more than reasonable."

"What did Dwight say?"

"He said you were partly to blame for the camera getting wrecked."

Paul swears and punches the dashboard.

"Hey, that's veneer, be careful," Joel says.

"Three days ago, you were telling me Dwight was a lying sack of shit. What makes you think he's telling the truth now?"

"I don't. But he is the director, and his word counts more than yours. Besides, he says he can manage the audio himself for the last week. It's not a blame thing, it's a budget thing. Trust me."

"So, you're saving seven hundred and fifty bucks by blaming me for the camera and firing me a week early. Is that it?"

"Don't look at it that way. You've done a great job. We'll work together again."

"How do you know I won't just grab my gear and leave?"

"Because I know you need the money."

Paul wonders if Joel will ask for the two thousand dollars back. He then remembers the envelope with the cash is still buried deep in the front pocket of his jeans. In his exhaustion and with all the madness, he'd forgotten about it, and Paul feels the edge of the envelope through the denim of his pants. To his credit, Joel doesn't say anything.

They arrive at the brewery. It looks like nothing happened, except the fire escape is now in the vacant lot next to the Porto Potty. Joel parks his Lexus behind the white van. Dwight waves, and Joel gets out of the car to shake his hand. Paul stays put in the Lexus for a full minute, watching the two men through the windshield. They were sworn enemies just 48 hours ago, and now they're allies. That's because they both want to get rid of him.

Good riddance, Paul thinks. He's getting off this damn shoot a week early. So, he'd make seven hundred and fifty less, but he still has the two thousand in blood money that Joel gave him. He'll put a fake smile on and get through the day. He is half-inclined to just grab his gear and walk away, but he does need the money, and Joel and Dwight still could maybe find a way to harm him.

Paul gets out of the Lexus as Joel slides back in. "Thanks Joel," Paul says.

"Stay in touch," he says, then starts the Lexus and is gone. *Stay in touch.* That's code for *we'll never see each other again.*

Paul puts his rig together without a word, and without looking at Victor or Dwight. The kids are already awake, so Paul and Victor nod at each other and go inside through the ground-floor metal door. This will be the last time I have to walk into this dump, Paul thinks.

Victor establishes the scene with some low wide shots. Jodi and Trent are arguing in the main room while Duncan watches from his newspaper-stuffed pallet. Ilima is in her new bedroom, passed out.

Victor goes into the back room and gets a tight face shot on Ilima. Her skin is grey and wet with sweat. Paul puts his boom microphone as close to the edge of the picture frame as he can and gets the sound of Ilima's tight labored breathing. She looks like she's dying.

Back in the main room Jodi slowly pulls off her black combat boots. She's not wearing socks and her feet are blistered, scabbed and bleeding.

"Fuck! I'm sick of this!" she yells, and throws her boots across the cement room. "These boots suck! This pain has GOT to stop."

Victor follows her into her room and gets an over-the-shoulder shot of Jodi pulling out a jewelry box. She opens the top and reveals the red velvet lining inside, along with buttons, pins, roach clips, earrings, and barrettes for her hair – the last remnants of a girlhood that Jodi once had long ago. Jodi pulls back the velvet lining and uncovers two long gold chains she'd hidden in the back. Victor trails Jodi back into the main room and gets a shot of her showing Trent the two chains. He tries to grab them, but she quickly pockets them.

"Why didn't you tell me you had those? Those are worth money."

"Because they belong to me. And I'm pawning them to buy a decent pair of shoes."

"Not looking like that, you won't," Trent warns.

"What's that supposed to mean?"

"Because you look like you need money so bad they'll give you a lousy price. You got to clean yourself up and dress nice."

They pull out the old suitcase that Duncan stole from the fat man in the train station and they fill it with all her dirty clothes. Duncan joins them like an obedient puppy. Then they count out five dollars in quarters that they had left over from spanging on Hollywood Boulevard and head out into the streets.

"What about Ilima?" Duncan asks.

"Let her sleep," Trent says. "That way she can get better."

Victor and Paul follow the trio as they lug the fat man's suitcase down the street, with Dwight keeping pace on the opposite sidewalk, chattering away into his walkie-talkie as he looks at his handheld monitor. They reach the Soaps and Suds Laundromat where they use all their quarters to wash her clothes.

"This better be worth it," Jodi says. "This is beer money."

Victor gets shots of the clothes going into the machine, close-ups of the quarters sliding into the coin slot and a dusting of soap going over her crusty yellowed underwear. He puts the camera in the dryer first and leaves it on, getting a shot of the clothes coming through the opening and covering the camera. Paul records the whir of the washer and the tumbling of the dryer.

They all help fold. They sniff the clean clothes and hold them to their faces, their brief warmth a deep comfort. Then they load up the suitcase and walk another four blocks to the Casa de Familias, a neighborhood shelter and legal center.

"I hate coming to this place," Trent says.

"I'm just taking a shower, I'll be out in fifteen minutes," Jodi says.

Jodi goes inside. Duncan and Trent cross the street, trying to be as far away from the other homeless people as possible. Paul can understand why. The homeless men who gather in front of the Casa are in bad shape, from crack, alcohol, mental illness and years of street living. The tribe is younger and healthier than these ghosts, and Trent and Duncan want nothing to do with them. Dwight stays twenty-five yards away and directs Victor to do long tracking shots of the homeless men across the street, and then over-the-shoulder and tight face shots of Trent and Duncan watching them.

A small woman in her 50s in a grey skirt and a white blouse exits the Casa and crosses the street towards Trent and Duncan. Victor steps to the side to catch her approach on camera, and the woman speaks right to the lens. "I don't give you permission to use my image for your TV show, so please don't point that camera at me."

Victor keeps rolling, so she kicks him hard in the shin with her pointed shoe. Victor stops shooting and hops on one foot, while she jabs a finger right in his face. "The men tell me you carry a gun and point it at them. If you come anywhere near the Casa with a gun, I'll have you all put in jail."

Dwight runs up, all smiles and apologies. "Sister McGinty! One of the kids is in the Casa taking a shower, that's the only reason why we're here."

"I'm glad. I want them all to take showers. That way I can convince them to get off the streets and away from you. Are you paying any of them yet?"

"Sister, it's a documentary. No one gets paid," Dwight says.

"What about you hiring some of the men off the street then? Give back to the community instead of taking?" She pokes her finger at Dwight now, the gold cross bouncing on the white blouse on her chest. Dwight backs away, and Paul can see that Dwight is intimidated by this small woman. Paul prepares to be attacked next, but she passes him over and goes straight for Trent.

"You sure you don't want to come in?"

He shakes his head. "We're not like these people."

"I know, you're children. So, let me help you," she asks, moving closer. Trent turns away from her and lights a cigarette as if she wasn't there.

"Don't you even think about blowing that smoke in my face," she says, poking him. "You think you're better than these people?"

"We're not old toothless crazy drug addicts. We can take care of ourselves."

"So then why aren't you in Hollywood with all the other runaways? That's where the youngsters are. You like the commute?"

"Maybe we just like the excitement of living downtown."

Sister McGinty takes out a pen and a card and scribbles on the back. "If you don't want to come here, there's the Night Shelter in Hollywood. You'll find a lot more people like you when you go there." She hands him the card. "That's the address, take it."

Trent does, and the Sister walks back across the street.

Five minutes later Jodi emerges, and her snow-white face and shock white hair is a contrast to the crowd of black men she must push through to get across the street.

"I'm clean, let's go," she mutters.

Back at the loft she opens the suitcase and takes off all her clothes, not caring who watches her. The tiny points of her breasts are the only curves in the taut white skin that stretches over her ribcage. Her pubic hair is a brown patch in a tiny triangle of white skin and jutting hip bones – a contrast to the white bleached hair on her head. Lit by one bare bulb hanging from the ceiling she is more famine victim than centerfold. Victor and Paul glance at each other only once, but Jodi sees it and laughs.

"Let's see you put this on TV," she sneers, and flexes her biceps for the camera.

She puts on clean underwear, a t-shirt, a blue denim skirt, a clean pink shirt from the fat man's suitcase, a beret over her spiked hair, tiny pink socks and Ilima's white platform 70s shoes. She grows four inches.

Trent hands her some lipstick and a broken hand mirror. "Go ahead, put it on."

Jodi paints her lips, then makes a gagging noise. She almost looks like the all-American suburban girl who she'd buried long ago.

"You look so normal," Duncan says.

"Fuck it," she says, "let's go make some money. I want me some new shoes."

Trent and Jodi head for the door, but when Duncan tries to follow them, Trent stops him. "Stay here and take care of Ilima," Trent says. "We'll only be gone a few hours." Duncan nods and sits back down.

A mad buzzing comes through Victor's headset. He pauses to listen, then motions for Paul to follow him. They dash back down the hall and scramble down the creaky fire escape, where Dwight waits with a small digital video camera.

"Paul – stay here and cover Duncan and Ilima with the small DV. I'll take your audio gear and follow Trent and Jodi to the pawnshop."

"I'm the only one allowed to use this gear."

"I'm the director, and I say it's fine," Dwight says.

"The insurance policy only covers me," Paul says. "If you mess it up I'm responsible for fixing it."

"I know how to run an audio rig," Dwight says.

"Why can't you cover Duncan and Ilima while Victor and I do the pawnshop?"

"Because I'm the director and that's not what I want. Now give me your rig."

Paul pauses. If he wanted something from Dwight – to borrow the camera to shoot something for his film, for instance – Dwight would never give it to him. That's because even after six weeks of shooting, Dwight still doesn't trust him and probably never will, yet he still insists that Paul trust *him* without question.

"I'll pay you the extra week you're losing, out of my own pocket. Okay? And I'm giving you a chance to shoot." Dwight laughs under his breath, like Paul is being a jerk.

Paul is trapped; Dwight acts like he's doing Paul a solid, and if he doesn't take him up on it, Dwight may still find a way to mess with him. What the hell, Paul thinks. There are only ten hours left of shooting and Big Andy has made his money back on his rig at least ten times over. By this point, Paul is so sick of Dwight and Victor and their condescending attitudes. He needs the extra money bad enough that he'll risk giving the rig to Dwight for a few hours.

He unclips the mixer and bag from his harness, then unzips his bag and pulls out a thick shoulder strap. He clips this onto the rig in two spots so Dwight can sling the whole contraption over his neck and shoulder. He hands the rig, headphones and the boom pole to Dwight, who then hands him a small DV camera.

Trent and Jodi walk by. Dwight heaves the rig onto his shoulder, picks up the boom pole, slides his headphones into place, and he and Victor dash after them. Paul stares at the camera in his hand. Should he do this? Why not? He heads back up the fire escape, twenty pounds lighter.

Paul stops in the doorway of the main room. Duncan paces like a bored tiger in a cage. Paul clicks the camera on. Duncan hears the noise and stops.

"Where's everybody else?"

"They're following Trent and Jodi. Just keep acting normal."

Duncan laughs. "Okay, I'll just keep acting normal." He goes back to pacing. "How's this? Does this look normal?"

Paul moves in close for a tight shot, but Duncan grabs the camera away.

"Come on, Duncan. Give it back."

Duncan holds the camera up to his eye and hits the record button, then walks forward until he is just an inch away from Paul's nose.

"It's your turn now," Duncan whispers. "Go on, just act normal."

Paul doesn't try grabbing the camera back. Instead, he walks over to the window where the setting sun will silhouette him. Duncan follows him, shooting the whole time – until the brightness of the background changes the shot so much he stops shooting.

"The iris ring is on the front. Just turn it a little and the background won't be so bright. Or see on the back? There's a green switch for 'automatic.' Turn that on and the camera automatically adjusts everything."

Duncan finds the switch and is pleased with the results.

"You can move to the side and try to make the light work for you too," Paul says. Instead Duncan swings low and shoots Paul from below.

"Do you like being filmed?" Duncan asks.

"It's tape, not film. And no, I don't like it."

"Now you know how it feels," Duncan smiles.

"Except you *love* being taped," Paul says.

"Yeah? How do you figure that?" Duncan asks.

"You always know where the camera is. You wait for the camera to swing around and land on you before you say anything. And you always know where the best light is."

Duncan smiles and lets the camera drop. "And I can tell that you hate Dwight and Victor, and they hate you. Right, Paul?"

Paul doesn't answer. He reaches for the camera, but Duncan won't let go.

"Why don't you go check on Ilima?" Paul asks. "I'll shoot it. That's something you want on tape, isn't it?"

Duncan stares at him for a long time, then releases the camera.

Paul takes it back and starts shooting. Duncan walks to Ilima's room and peeks in. It's dark inside, so Paul motions to Duncan to light some candles. Duncan goes around the room, slowly lighting candle after candle, letting Paul move in for each shot. The room full of lit candles makes for a wonderful shot. Duncan kneels on the floor next to the dirty mattress and touches Ilima's face.

This shot is fantastic, Paul thinks. He feels his stomach leap and turn at the same time. It is a fantastic shot, and it looks good because he directed it, even suggesting that Duncan go visit Ilima and then light the candles. However, it's not the natural "fly-on-the-wall" footage that Dwight wants. Good as it might be, Paul is only getting the shot because he crossed Dwight's purity line, so Dwight will never use it.

Duncan sits next to Ilima on the bed and strokes her sweaty face. Duncan finds a shirt and dabs up the perspiration, holding a candle to give Paul even more light to shoot. Ilima opens her eyes and smiles. "Can I have some water?"

Duncan leaves and comes back with water while Paul keeps shooting. She sits up and sips from a cup, then coughs. Duncan holds the shirt under her chin as she spits up a green grey chunk of phlegm.

"Yuck. You're really sick."

"At least I'm losing weight, right?" she laughs.

"You should change your clothes, you're all wet," Duncan says. He digs through her pile and comes back with a sweatshirt. He pulls her shirt off, along with the yellow bikini top she uses as a bra, letting her breasts flop free. Ilima is too drained to object and just allows Duncan to dress her.

"Wow, you must be sick. Usually you'd slap me about now."

He gives her another sip of water then tucks her back under the covers. Paul moves in for the tight shot. He starts on a close-up of Duncan, who leans down and kisses Ilima on the forehead. Paul tilts down and ends up a close-up of Ilima smiling.

"I think I'm ready to go to the hospital now. I want a real hospital room, with TV and Jell-O."

"I'll tell Trent when he gets back," Duncan says.

"I can't wait. Besides, he'll say 'no.' You can take me, can't you?"

"We don't have any money to pay. Trent says they'll just give you pills and make you go away."

Paul remembers the two thousand dollars in his pocket. Ilima is sick enough that they'll give her a hospital room, even if they are destitute. They might have to pay a little money, but not much, and these kids don't know that. If Duncan doesn't do anything, Ilima might die of pneumonia like Jim Henson, the guy who created the Muppets, who died after being a lot less sick. This is also Paul's last day, and he knows that Dwight and Victor won't do anything to help her. It's him, or nobody.

Paul puts the camera down, goes into the main room and retrieves the old suitcase. He pulls out the two thousand dollars from his front pocket, kicks open the suitcase and puts the cash in the zippered silk corner pocket.

When he turns back around, Duncan is watching him. "There's two thousand dollars in there, for you and Ilima, Trent and Jodi. That's enough to take Ilima to the hospital, and enough to help everybody change their lives. It's yours, so take it. Then show it to Ilima and tell her what I just told you. Then take her to the hospital."

Duncan nods. Paul picks up his camera, and Duncan does precisely what he was told. Paul shoots him unzipping the pouch and taking out the wad of money. He then goes back to Ilima and shows her the cash. "This is two thousand dollars, for you and me. That's enough to take you to the hospital, and enough to help us change our lives."

Ilima smiles and touches his face. A tear rolls down her cheek.

Paul grabs the close-up of the tear, then backs up for the wide shot. Duncan scoops her up off the dirty mattress, blanket and all. Paul backpedals out of the room as Duncan walks towards him, carrying Ilima like a rag doll. They follow Paul down the stairs and out the unlocked front metal door and out into the street.

"Don't get too far ahead, this microphone isn't any good past a few feet," Paul whispers. Duncan barely nods with his chin held high and his eyes forward. He looks heroic. They walk two blocks to a payphone. Duncan kneels on one knee, rests Ilima on the other, then reaches up for the receiver and dials 911.

"I need an ambulance. My best friend is sick," he says, and looks down at her. She gazes back up at him with adoration. Paul captures it all on tape.

The ambulance arrives in eight minutes with sirens blaring. Ilima faints as Duncan lifts her back into his arms. He holds her out to the paramedics rushing to meet them. One checks her temperature and takes her pulse while the other asks questions.

"What's wrong with her?"

"She's been sick for a long time. She's coughing up blood," Duncan says.

Paul keeps shooting, always circling, moving in closer, ending on a tight shot of Ilima's face as they lay her head down on the emergency gurney.

"Pulse is 160 and thin," one paramedic says.

"Pupils are dilated, labored breathing – she's got an obstruction in her lungs, or that's one hell of an infection."

"Radio it in."

They push the gurney into the ambulance, Duncan jumps in, the doors shut, and the paramedics are back in their cab before Paul can even think to ask to ride along.

"There's no room. She'll be in St. Luke's Emergency," the driver says.

The ambulance takes off. Paul rests on the shot of the receding ambulance, sirens blaring, letting it get smaller in the frame, until it rounds the corner and disappears.

Paul shuts the camera off and looks around. The street is empty. Dwight and Victor are still out following Jodi and Trent as they sell jewelry and buy shoes. After five weeks of working eighteen hours a day, here he is, on his last day of shooting with three hours left on his schedule and absolutely nothing to do.

Paul thinks about leaving. His job is done, and his last paycheck will be in the mail on Friday. He wants to leave the camera in the kids' main room in the vats and just go, but Dwight took the audio rig.

Paul walks back to the brewery and sits down next to the panel van. He wants to wait in the van on Victor's cot, but he doesn't have keys. He sits on the curb and ejects the tape from the camera. He looks at it and wonders whether he should rewind and erase the beginning of it, where he breaks the rules and talks to Duncan.

Screw it, let him see it. He slides it in his jacket pocket.

Two hours later, he spots Trent and Jodi coming around the corner with Victor and Dwight trailing after them. From this distance, he can see how absurd the whole arrangement is – two homeless kids walking along while one guy with a $50,000 camera creeps alongside, while another guy extends what looks like furry roadkill on a stick over their heads. There is nothing real about any of it.

As they come closer, he can see that Jodi wears brand new red boots, and she has already scuffed them up as best she can. Victor gets a low tracking shot of the kids as they come around the corner of the building. Victor and Dwight spot Paul and stop.

"Where are Duncan and Ilima?"

"Duncan took Ilima to the hospital. The ambulance picked them up two hours ago. But don't worry, I got the whole thing on the DV camera."

Dwight's face turns purple. He takes Big Andy's audio rig off his shoulder and throws it against the curb, then snaps the $800 boom handle across his knee.

"That's for the camera. Now we're even." Dwight says.

Paul looks at Dwight, then looks at the damaged rig and wonders if he'll end up paying for it. He hands the DV camera back to Dwight.

"I only have an hour left, so I'll leave early. You can send me Jodi and Trent's microphones later. Nice working with you guys."

Paul collapses the pieces of the broken boom pole as best he can, then picks up the damaged rig and heads off down the street. He expects Dwight or Victor to come chasing after him, either to apologize and or to attack him, but they don't.

They'll chase me soon enough. Because now he has something they all want to see. He has the DV tape of the ending of the documentary that Joel wants so badly. He turns the corner, stops, and pulls the small digital videotape from his pocket. He holds it up to the setting sun. He doesn't know where this tape will lead him, but he's moving into uncharted territory.

CHAPTER 17

P aul sleeps for three days straight, only getting up to eat, shower, and go to the bathroom. Maggie spends those nights on the couch, so he can sleep better, only coming in to see if he's breathing. In the morning, he hears quiet puttering – coffee cup, toothbrush, keys and the door – before the sound of her car fades away and he drifts back to sleep.

On the afternoon of the third day he bolts awake and looks at his watch, terrified that it's 5:30 p.m., then realizes he doesn't have to be anywhere. He lies back down and grins. The nightmare is finally over. He doesn't have to catch a bus, he doesn't have to carry a boom pole until his shoulders ache, or endure Dwight yelling at him. No more punk clubs, bus rides, pancake houses, squat fires, and no more homeless kids.

He wonders how the kids are doing. He doesn't regret giving Duncan the money, but now he realizes just how badly he needed that extra two thousand dollars. He made less than the five thousand he'd anticipated. Dwight ruined Andy's expensive gear, but he should have insurance, so he's probably safe there. But if he pays Maggie back first, that leaves him short for the car payments and the credit cards. And his film? That will be locked in the lab for years, at this rate.

Damn. Except for some vivid movie moments for the mental file drawer, he is back to the same existence he always has had; looking for work while hiding from creditors and the repo men.

He thinks about the DV tape sitting in his desk drawer, with the footage he shot of Duncan carrying Ilima, calling 911, and the paramedics loading her onto the gurney and into the ambulance and then driving away. It's the only proof he has that it happened. He knows they'll call soon, unless Dwight is too proud to ever use the footage he shot.

Paul cleans the apartment and cooks dinner. He opts for a stir-fry concoction with rice, and opens a bottle of wine. Tonight, they'll have a "talk," and for that, they'll need wine. Lots of wine.

Paul can't tell where her head is at. The last two mornings she left for work like she always does, but she no longer rewards him with long gazes or punishes him with extended pouts. She just moves from room to room while he gazes at her. She is the enigma now, not him, and it's unsettling.

Has she decided it's over? Is she planning her exit? He hears the stereo go on in Rupert's apartment upstairs. He doesn't want to think about the pompous Englishman and what might have happened. He lights candles for dinner and pours two glasses of wine.

Maggie walks in, breathless.

"Good timing," Paul says. "You just have time for a glass of wine before dinner."

She drops her bags, sips her wine, and watches him stir the rice.

"Look at you, Mr. Homebody. Do you do windows too?"

"Ask, and you shall receive."

"Oh, goody. I'll make a list. Let's see, caulking in the kitchen, grout the bathroom, polish the wood floors, clean under the refrigerator... "

He presses against her, wooden spoon in hand. "Housework? Is that all that's on that list?"

She doesn't giggle or push him away, but meets his gaze. She knits her brow and examines him closely, switching from eye to eye. He chooses her left eye to focus on and watches her pupil dilate, like a camera lens opening.

"See anything real in there?" he asks. "Is there truth in this soul?" She purses her lips but doesn't answer. "Let's eat."

Dinner and three glasses of wine and one Al Green album later, Paul still waits for her to bring it up. He hates that. They both know what's going on, and she is making *him* bring it up.

Paul remembers a phrase that Andy uses that summed up this romantic situation: "He who cares less, wins." And right now, Maggie cares less about having a talk than he does, so he'll have to do all the work.

"Earth to Paul," Maggie says.

"Huh?"

"You've been staring at that candle for five minutes."

"Five minutes? More like two."

"Fine, two minutes. I'll do the dishes." She gets up.

"Wait." He grabs her wrist.

She yanks it away. "Don't grab me like that."

"Calm down, I just touched you."

"You grabbed my wrist while I had dishes in my hands. I don't like being grabbed, so don't do it."

"I'm not some stranger in the street threatening you. Stop overreacting."

"No, you grabbing me is overreacting. We're in a tiny apartment, I'm not going anywhere. If you want my attention, use your voice and ask."

Paul closes his eyes and exhales slowly. "This is getting off to a bad start."

"You got that right."

"I'd like you to sit down again so we can talk."

Maggie sits back down and puts her hands up in surrender. "I'm ready to talk."

"Now that the job's over I want to discuss where you and I stand."

"Are you asking whether I think we should continue this relationship?"

"Yes."

"It depends on what your plans are," she asks.

"My plans haven't changed. I want to finish my film somehow."

"Then we have a problem," she says.

"How is wanting to finish my film a problem?"

"Because you're not living in reality. You must get a job, get out of debt, and *then* find the money and time to finish a film you've been working on for three years. And once it's done, this film will then do what for you? Will it change your life?"

"I don't know what it will do. I just know I have to try."

"You're living in some dream world of what might happen to you, while life is passing you by. Meanwhile, my life is passing me by too. We've never taken a vacation together, not even a weekend trip. Do you realize that?"

"You want me to give it up? You know how much I love film."

"Well, it doesn't love you. You haven't even worked on a film job in months. You're doing hard labor on crap TV that are going to air once and then disappear."

"You don't know that."

"You said yourself that this reality show was a waste of your time. There's nothing real about it."

"That car accident was real. The assault. The fire. The eighteen-hour days."

Maggie sighs and touches her temples. "I know. That's not what I meant."

"And that girl really was sick. There was more real life going on in that brewery than in your office building. And Duncan trusted me. I liked him, and he liked me. We had a real connection there, no matter how lame the TV show is."

Maggie reaches out across the table and holds his hands. "Paul, you're smart and you work hard. You would've succeeded ten times over in any other career by now. Give it a break."

Paul sees something in her eyes he'd never seen before. Pity. She pities him.

"Are you making me choose between you and my film?"

"That's very dramatic, but I didn't say that." Maggie gets up, goes to the coffee machine and fills up the filter with coffee, facing away from him. "I'm saying that I want you to pay me back for rent and groceries, and set money aside for a vacation. For that you need a real job."

"I can write you a check right now." Paul jumps up and goes to the writing desk, pulls out his checkbook and scribbles her a check for the back rent and groceries.

She fills the machine with water, hits the red button and turns to face him again. "And I want you to pay half the rent and half the bills from now on. I also want you to make the creditors stop calling, and I want to park my own car in my own garage. I want all this to happen by the first of the month."

"That's in less than three weeks."

"It's exactly twenty days. I'm not saying I want to break up with you. But if you can't do it by then I want you to move out." The coffee machine bubbles and clicks. Maggie pours herself a cup and adds milk.

"That's not much time."

"You can do it."

Paul grabs the newspaper out of the recycling pile and finds the want ads.

"What are you doing?"

"Looking for a real job. I don't have much time."

CHAPTER 18

P aul gets a job as a tape librarian at a video editing facility called Premier Video. His job description is listed on a piece of paper stuck to the wall:

*To all Premier Video Tape Libarians (*yes, this is how they spell it)

1) No food or drink in the tape libary (yes, the librarian misspelled the word *library*).

2) Label incoming client tapes with bar code stickers and register them into the computer. Place bar code stickers on both the box and the tape! Or Hank will kill you!

3) Check the schedule sheet when you come in, then check in with Hank.

4) Fifteen minutes before each session load all the client tapes for the project on a cart and place the cart in the edit suite for that project. Don't fuck it up.

5) After each session, take the cart back to the libary and put the tapes back on the shelves. Don't fuck it up.

Hank is the post production coordinator for Premier Video and is five feet three inches tall, bald, and very angry. He gives Paul a brief lesson on bar codes, then tells Paul to do whatever the Zigster and Manuel command him to do.

Paul is the newest of three tape librarians (the Zigster and Manuel being the other two) and is therefore the low man on the totem pole. He earns ten dollars an hour to work ten hours a day in a sealed vault with no windows, under fluorescent lighting. Manuel, a student at Cal State Northridge, is on a fast track to move into the dubbing room. The Zigster is a part-time student at the Rock and Roll Music School in Hollywood and has plans to be a rock guitar god. There is a suction fan in the vault that helps keep the room clean from dust and debris, and whenever work is slow The Zigster will stand next to the air uptake, light a joint and smoke out. Hank never smells it.

Paul worked in the tape vault for two weeks and took home $900 after taxes. He used $200 to pay for groceries and bills and he paid $700 towards his $22,000 credit card debt. That may be enough to make the creditors stop calling. That's two of the four requirements. But he still owes Maggie for the coming month's rent, plus he hasn't paid any past due car payments yet, so he can't give Maggie her garage back. If he doesn't find a way to fulfill the last two requirements, he may be out on the street in a week.

The boys in the Cutlass now trail him to work, screaming obscenities at him while he waits at the bus stop. "You're a loser, Franti! Fuck you! You work in a tape vault!"

"I'll have the money for you in a week," he pleads.

"Suck my dick, faggot! You can't even afford a car!"

They tried harassing Maggie once as she left the apartment, but she called the police. A squad car came, but the cops let them off with a warning. She then went to her boss, the Screaming Asshole, and told him about the situation, and the Screaming Asshole (to his credit) put his company lawyer on it and had a restraining order placed against both men. The Screaming Asshole then demanded sex from her, and she laughed and pretended he was just joking.

Paul calls his mom in Andover, Massachusetts for money, but she can only give him $250, and his dad in Florida tells him on the phone that Paul needs to go through this alone to "learn about character."

"Thanks, Dad. And say 'hi' to your former secretary who's now my stepmom. I learned a lot about character when you made that move," Paul says, and hangs up.

He needs a miracle. He thinks of the DV tape in the drawer. He thought he'd have cashed in that chip by now, but that seems like a longshot now.

When Maggie is home, there is an uneasy sense of the looming deadline. Maggie is friendly but distant, which makes Paul think that she believes he won't make it. They do sleep in the same bed, however, and they even have sex once – but with no giggling, cuddling, or cooing silliness, and it ends with a peck on the lips before Maggie jumps out of bed for work. Paul feels like a visiting "friend with benefits" who stays a few days before being asked to move on.

The person who is most sympathetic is Big Andy, who feels bad for introducing Paul to Joel in the first place. Even though Andy's gear was destroyed, he made good money on the rental. The gear was also insured, but Joel Cuvney hasn't signed the paperwork and isn't returning Andy's phone calls, so Andy doesn't expect to see a claim check anytime soon. Joel may be delaying out of spite, or he has legal problems with the show and the network is preventing him from signing.

"I'll make it up to you, I swear," Paul says.

"Don't worry about it. It taught me that I shouldn't be in the gear rental business."

Andy buys Paul lunch at the Cat and Fiddle pub and restaurant on Sunset Boulevard. Paul has a 45-minute break for lunch, which suits Andy fine because he has another meeting at Capitol Records with XXX-Tra and their management. Andy leans back and stretches his arms, his new leather jacket squeaking on his big frame. He is all smiles.

"They signed a contract with me guaranteeing that I'd produce their next two albums. That's why I gave them studio time and produced their first record for free. Now that the record company loves them, they want to put in their own producer and squeeze me out," Andy says.

"What are you going to do?"

"My lawyer is on it. I'm going to get a percentage of ownership of those fuckers."

"Do you think you'll get it?"

"Oh yeah. My contract is ironclad. I saw this coming a while ago."

"My problem is I never see anything coming."

"You're doing okay. Better than those homeless kids you were following."

"This is true," Paul says and means it. The tribe is still out there somewhere, fighting to find food, and he'd just eaten a decent meal in the warm sun. He flashes back to one of the hundred nights of shooting, when Trent led them to a big blue dumpster behind a Chinese restaurant in Hollywood. Duncan dived in and found a bucket of fried rice and noodles. The tribe was happy that night.

Paul puts his dark glasses on and picks at his damp French fries. "I better get back to the vault. We're on-lining some 'Survivor' promos in an hour."

Andy tosses down a fifty-dollar bill and puts on his glasses. "Paul, if a decent job comes up at the recording studio, it's yours."

"Thanks."

The two men shake hands, and Paul is aware that if they stay on their respective courses they won't be having very many more of these lunches.

Andy's cell phone rings and he answers. "Hello?"

Paul pats him on the back and walks away, until Andy grabs him and motions at the phone.

"Joel Cuvney! How are you, sir? I hope Paul and the gear served you well on your project? Good! Yeah, I heard about the damage, no problem, no problem, I'm sure you're good for it."

Paul gestures that he has had enough and keeps walking, but Andy grabs him by the collar and yanks him back into the restaurant. "As a matter of fact, he's right here with me. We just finished lunch. Hang on," Andy says, and hands the phone to Paul and threatens to hit him if he doesn't talk.

"Hello?"

"Paul? It's me Joel. I really need your help."

CHAPTER 19

Joel tells Paul to meet him in the Souplantation restaurant on Third Street. Paul finds him in a side booth nursing a bowl of clam chowder and a side salad. Joel jumps to his feet and pumps his hand. He's wearing a tracksuit and hasn't shaved in weeks.

"Paul! Thanks for coming. Do you want anything? Grab a tray and help yourself. The corn bread here is amazing."

"That's okay, I just ate."

Joel sits back down and digs in with his spoon. "I know what you're thinking – I'm eating food off a *tray*. Normally I wouldn't be caught dead in a place like this, but now I'm eating three meals a day in here. That's how bad things have gotten. Seven days a week, for weeks now. I'm a regular here, along with all the retirees. I have the whole fucking menu memorized."

"So where are you editing?"

"Next door, in the Third Street Executive Suites. Ever been in there?"

"Oh yeah, many times," Paul says. "I call it the Habitrail."

Joel pushes his tray away and rubs his eyes. "I sit in that edit bay with that prick Dwight and the editor fifteen hours a day, except when I escape in here to wolf down my food and go back. You can't imagine what it's like."

"Yes, I can. I worked with Dwight eighteen hours a day doing audio, remember?"

Joel dismisses him with a wave of his hand. "That's different. At least you were moving around. I'm in a tiny dark room with two assholes who both think they're geniuses, looking at tape after tape, cut after cut, and it never ends. And all we need is ninety minutes. It's hell, Paul. I swear to God, it's just like that play that French guy wrote."

"*No Exit.*"

"That right, *No Exit.* Except I do get to leave three times a day to listen to the canned Lionel Ritchie music here in the Souplantation."

Paul decides not to tell him about his current job working in the tape vault. He had to pay The Zigster twenty dollars to cover for him this afternoon.

"Have you heard anything from the kids?" Paul asks.

"What kids?" Joel asks with his mouth full, honestly confused.

"The ones you're doing a show about? Remember them?"

"I didn't know who you were talking about. I hardly think of them as kids."

"Do you know where they are?"

"Nope. We paid Ilima's hospital bills and I paid off that kid Xander again for a second surgery. Then they disappeared. That's the last I heard from any of them. The city still doesn't know we were shooting there." Joel waves his hands in front of his face. "Poof! It's like it never even happened."

"Except for those two thousand tapes in there."

"Don't remind me." Joel hangs his head in his hands.

"Don't you wonder about them? Even a little bit?" Paul asks.

Joel shakes his head. "Not in the least. Do you?"

"Yeah. I wonder if they're okay."

"I just want this project to be over." Joel hangs his head in his hands again.

"So how far are you in editing? Do you have a rough cut yet?"

"We've got three rough cuts, all different and they all suck. They're *boring.*"

"It was a pretty boring shoot most of the time," Paul says.

"Fine, so it was boring! You take all the boring stuff out and keep the interesting stuff! That's editing, right? The verb is 'to edit,' to remove! Dwight's in there in love with every tiny nuance in that damn pancake house. He edits these long montages where they just stare off into space and do NOTHING. He says he's trying to capture their hopelessness."

"What about the fight with Xander? Or the begging on Hollywood Boulevard, or Jodi and Trent having sex, or Ilima being sick?"

Joel raises his arms in frustration. "I have two thousand tapes in there. I have no idea where any of that is. And even if I found it, I can't force Dwight to use any of it."

"What about the editor? Who's he?"

"Rick Raden. He edited two seasons of *Survivor*. He edited all the team competitions, that was his specialty."

"Is he any good?"

"I have no idea," Joel says, shaking his head. "Everything he edits Dwight changes anyway. He came in excited, but he's so beaten down he's just pushing the buttons now. For weeks Dwight hovered in his chair behind him, literally breathing down his neck. It got so bad that Rick put a piece of white tape on the ground and said if Dwight ever crossed it again, he'd kill him."

"I'm surprised he hasn't quit."

"He wants to, but the holidays are coming up and there's not a lot of people hiring right now. I heard him on his cell phone in the garage. He's just putting in his time until he gets another gig. He's got some *Survivor* spinoff that starts in January."

Joel rests his face in his hands and sighs. Paul looks around the restaurant. It's still busy, even though it's close to three o'clock. Back at the tape vault, Hank is probably just noticing that he is gone, and Paul is hoping that The Zigster is a decent paid liar. If Joel doesn't offer him something, Paul may not salvage the one job he does have.

That's when Paul notices that Joel is asleep, propped up on his elbows with his head still in his hands. Paul taps him on the knuckles with a spoon and Joel snorts awake.

"Sorry. I'm back."

"I have to get back to work."

"Work? You're working? Since when are you working?" Joel seems stunned, which pisses Paul off.

"Since when? Since I have bills and rent due like everyone else, so I found a job. And I took time off work to come here to listen to you, but now I have to get back."

Paul stands up to leave and Joel grabs his arm. "You can't go back to work. You have to work for me."

"As what?"

"As an assistant editor."

Paul shakes his head and walks out. He blinks away his fury while searching his pockets for bus fare, when Joel catches up with him.

"Wait, wait, wait," Joel says, grabbing his arm. "I didn't mean it that way. I'll call you by that title, but you'll be doing a lot more than that."

"I've already had a better job with you, and you fired me," Paul says. He tries to get on the bus, but Joel grabs him off the bottom step and waves for the driver to move on.

"You're pissing me off, Joel," Paul says. "I don't need this anymore."

"Yes, you do! I have a plan. Just listen to this – I fire Rick. I have to, he's just punching a clock right now. Then I tell Dwight he can edit the show himself, any way he wants. Then I hire you as *his* assistant editor, just digitizing footage and arranging material for him. It makes sense, because you know the footage and can find it a lot easier than Rick could."

"I don't want to be in the same room as Dwight," Paul says.

"You don't have to be! You'll be in another room preparing material for him to work on, and in the edit bay when he's not there."

Paul shrugs. "I have no desire to help Dwight on his show. I'd rather just forget the whole thing ever happened."

Joel smiles. "But that's only half the job. I've just rented another editing system on the other end of the building that Dwight doesn't know about. When you're not digitizing material for him, I want you to be working in the other bay, editing the show the way *you* think it should be, like we talked about."

"You want me to cut a different show behind Dwight's back?"

Joel neither says yes or no, he just shrugs. "I have a contractual obligation to give Dwight sixteen weeks of editing time to deliver the cut he wants. I'm doing that right now. But the network owns the footage, not Dwight, and I have an obligation to deliver the best show possible. You know the footage and you're a filmmaker. I think you're the only person who can deliver that show for me."

Paul sits down on the bus stop bench to think. The sky is dark blue with white clouds moving in a crisp autumn breeze. Paul missed the joys of summer while doing audio for Dwight, and now he's missing beautiful autumn days like today, locked in that vault. Then again, if he takes Joel up on his offer he'll be locked away in a dark edit room, cut off from the outside world again, never seeing the sun or a blue sky filled with marching clouds.

Paul watches a cloud disappear behind the Beverly Center and his reverie ends. He turns to Joel.

"What's the salary, and what's the credit?"

"The salary is $1800 a week," Joel answers.

"I need $3000 a week."

"But you've never edited a network show," Joel says. "That's not fair."

"You just said I was the only person in the world who could do this for you."

"I'll pay you $2500 a week. No more."

"I want $2750 for every five days of work. That's $550 a day, no matter what. If I work ten days straight, that's $5500. And if my version airs, I need story-editing, editing, and co-producer credits. And I need that written down in a contract."

Joel smiles. "If you write it up, I'll make a contract, sign it and send it to the network honchos and make it happen." Joel sticks out his hand and the two men shake. "You'll have your name on as an editor, story editor, producer – whatever you want."

"If I decide to take the job, you'll get my write-up tomorrow."

"Do it and you can start work the next day."

Paul nods. It's not film, it's not stellar material, but it's a real show, for a real network. It would be Hell, but no worse than the other hells he's endured already. But what's most important is that he'll be able, in one week, to pay Maggie everything he owes for the coming month and – just maybe – pay enough back car payments to make the repo men go away. But going back into Hell won't be easy, and he must convince Maggie; after all, this is not the job she envisioned for him when she gave him her ultimatum.

He thought of the DV tape. This might be his chance to use it.

CHAPTER 20

Maggie shakes her head and laughs under her breath. "I thought you didn't trust Joel."

"I don't," Paul says, "but I don't trust Hank, the head of the tape vault, either. And I think I'd rather get screwed over while editing a network special than screwed over while working as a tape librarian."

"Sounds shady to me, if you want my opinion."

Paul does want her opinion, just as long as it matches his. He watches her unload groceries from a line of paper bags on the kitchen counter. She tosses soup cans on shelves, milk in the refrigerator, and garbage bags under the sink, while her hips and feet shut drawers and slam cabinets.

"Do you need help?"

"No, I have a system. Isn't it nice to finally have decent food in the house? And to have the time to enjoy it?"

"God, yes. I never want to see macaroni and cheese or Top Ramen again."

"And I have a special surprise to end the evening."

She tears open the last two bags and reveals two orange pumpkins.

"Ta da! We can carve them for Halloween," she announced. "It's in two days."

"We live in an apartment with a gated courtyard. We're not going to get trick or treaters," Paul complains.

"I bought them for us," she points out. She walks around the edge of the counter and tugs on his shirtfront. "What else were we going to do tonight? Watch TV? Go to another movie? Let's do something real, in the here and now. Come on, it'll be fun."

Paul smiles and kisses her. "I'll lay out newspapers."

She's right, Paul thinks. He needs a change, and this may finally be it.

He'd rather not go back to work in the vault. He didn't get back from his meeting with Joel until 3:30 in the afternoon, and Hank caught him walking in the door.

"I had a dentist's appointment," he lied.

"You haven't worked here long enough to have dentist appointments. Do it again, and you're fired."

Paul almost quit right then to take Joel's offer, but decided to think things over with Maggie before jumping back into the raging ocean of TV production. He is proud of himself for maintaining his composure, but he's sure leaning to taking the job.

Maggie digs through the kitchen drawers. "A small blade with a serrated edge works best. I remember that from when I was little."

"Yeah, almost like a grapefruit knife."

Maggie brings two small steak knives to the table, along with two Sharpies and a stack of paper. "Which way do you swing for your jack-o-lantern? Funny or scary?"

"Scary."

"You go scary, I'll do something funny."

They ruin a half tablet of copy paper testing and rejecting ideas, starting with the traditional face with the triangle eyes and nose. Then they move through the sexy girl winking, the shocked face with the open mouth, the face with the leering grin, and the bashful face glancing to the side.

"Who does this look like to you?" Maggie asks, holding up a design. The face is smug, with a raised eyebrow and tiny smirk. Paul shrugs.

"It's Joel."

Paul laughs. "That's perfect! When did you ever see Joel?"

"I found his picture at TheHollywoodReporter.com."

"If you're going to do Joel, then I have to do Dwight." Paul scribbles out a screaming face with bulging eyes and with flame trails coming out of his nose, ears and mouth. He holds it up for her assessment.

"Ouch, scary! I think we have our designs!"

They carefully copy their designs onto the orange skin of their respective pumpkins and then carve out the tops. They jam their hands into the gooey white fibers inside and dribble out the guts and seeds onto the newspapers, filling the apartment with a sweet pumpkin scent. Paul threatens to touch Maggie with a slimy hand.

"Don't you dare," she warns him, but he goes ahead and sticks a wet seed to her forehead. She laughs and slimes him with a hand across his cheek.

When they're done carving, they drop votive candles inside each pumpkin and Paul lights them with a kitchen match held between tongs. He goes to the light switch. "Ready?"

Maggie leans back on the couch. He flicks the switch, sending the apartment into pitch darkness except for the eerie glow from the pumpkins. He joins her on the couch and they admire their handiwork.

"They look great," Maggie says. "One looks like he's really condescending and the other looks like he's really screaming."

"I guess we should call them Joel-o-lantern, and Dwight-o-lantern."

Maggie snuggles close to him. "Are you really going to take this job?"

"I think so," Paul says. "I'm too old to be working in a tape vault. Besides, the money's too good to pass up. I can pay my share of rent and the bills, and give you your garage back."

"Are you going to work crazy hours again?"

"Probably. But if I work six weeks, I can also pay off the rest of the car payments, plus a big chunk of my credit card bill. Then I can pay the lab and get my film back. I'll be at square one."

Maggie sits up on the couch and faces him. The orange light from the jack-o-lanterns dances across the right side of her face, while the left is in pitch darkness.

"Square one isn't moving forward. I want you to get a real job, one that doesn't end in six weeks. That's what grown-ups do."

"I'm a grown-up."

"You believe that?"

I'll tell you what. I won't worry about paying off my film and credit card until later. I'll save money, and when this job is done we'll take a two-week vacation. Then when I get back I'll stop all this madness and get a real job. You can ask for vacation time at work tomorrow."

"You promise?"

"You said taking a vacation proves we're grown-ups, right? We'll go to Cabo San Lucas or Hawaii, wherever you want."

She kisses him long and hard and pushes him back against the couch. They make out in the candlelight. Her hands creep up under his shirt and across his stomach.

"Hello, Mr. Six Pack. When have you been working out?"

"It's all the boxes I've been lifting at work."

"You sure you want that editing job? I think I like you better this way."

His hands creep up under her shirt, unsnaps the front of her bra, and strokes each nipple. She pulls back quickly.

"Your hands are cold."

"Let's warm them up in the bedroom," he says, and starts to pull her off the couch. She stops him.

"I only have one question about this job, and then I'll shut up. You said you'd never ever work with Dwight again."

"I won't be working with Dwight. I'll be preparing work for him to edit."

"So, you're assistant editing, you're not editing."

"I'll be assistant-editing for Dwight for just a few hours a day, prepping footage in another edit bay. Then Joel will have me edit a different version for him on the sly in another edit bay on the other end of the building."

Maggie pulls her hand away and sits back down. She stares at Paul. "You and Joel are going behind Dwight's back?"

Paul shrugs. "I guess so. But I don't care about Dwight. It's not his show. He's not paying for it, the network is. And Joel's the producer. I'm working for Joel now."

"Dwight's no dummy. He'll find out what you're doing. And when he does, he is going to be pissed."

"Good," Paul says. "I'll be looking forward to it." He blows out the candles and falls back onto the couch, pinning her against the cushions. He kisses her forehead. He can barely see the outline of Maggie's face in the darkness.

"Just be careful. People like him turn crazy really quick."

CHAPTER 21

The room is 10 feet by 10 feet with grey carpet. The editing system includes two monitors, a computer, two tape decks, a mixing board, a CD player, and an audio interface system, with just enough room for a bookcase, two chairs, a lamp, and a denim couch against the back wall. Joel put up posters to make the room feel homey – one of the Beatles and another of a pregnant Arnold Schwarzenegger from the movie *Junior*.

Paul sits in the edit chair waiting for Joel and Dwight to come in. He first met them in Joel's office months ago in Century City, and here he is again, nervously waiting for them to appear. He touches the top of his head and feels the raised ridge of the scar under his hairline. His hair has returned along with his health, but Paul has a sinking feeling that might change again soon.

The door swings open and Joel and Dwight walks in. Dwight grins and offers his hand like an old pal. "Paul, I'm glad to have you back. I hope there are no hard feelings."

"I have some, but Joel's paying me enough to get over them. Plus, he finally signed the paperwork, so Andy can file an insurance claim on the gear you destroyed."

Joel and Dwight throw their heads back and laugh too loud, as if he were joking. Dwight pats him on the back. "That's a good one! I must say, I had my doubts about the audio that you were doing, but it's a lot better than I expected. Most of the time I can actually edit a scene with your stuff."

Paul decides to ignore the backhanded compliment and changes the subject. "Have you heard anything from the kids?"

"The tribe split up. Ilima got out of the hospital and moved in with a cousin down in Orange County. She's fine now. Trent and Jodi are still together, living with some people in a one-room apartment in Hollywood. I have no idea where Duncan is. He's out there somewhere, being Duncan."

"What about Victor?"

"The mad Russian? He's shooting that show *Face Your Fears* for CBS. He climbs into some big pit with a camera and shoots terrified people covered in padding fighting off a pack of wild dogs. It's perfect for him."

Paul waits. He thinks for sure Dwight will ask him for the DV tape he took from the camera on the last shooting day, but Dwight doesn't mention it. He must not want anything "false" that Paul shot polluting his project. All Paul knows is that he's sure going to put it in his version of the show, when he gets a chance.

Joel steps in and looks at his watch. "Should we get started? I'll get the coffee, there's a Starbucks across the street."

"No corporate coffee for me," Dwight says, "around here I only buy coffee from the Arab market on the corner. Paul smiles and nods that he'll have one too.

An hour later Paul sits in the editor's seat. He stares at the screen, trying to understand how the project is organized. Dwight sits in the seat next to him, and Joel sprawls on the couch behind them, while the steam from their tall paper cups fills the room with the strong smell of coffee and sugar.

Paul uses the mouse to scroll through Dwight's work so far, watching the different scenes he and his editor have cut. Dwight points at the screen, indicating which icons to click to play the scenes that he likes. He keeps moving closer to Paul, until Dwight hovers over Paul's shoulder. Paul feels like he is in the front seat of a two-man bobsled. Dwight even places his hand over Paul's hand on the mouse, his need to control him is that strong.

"Click on 'Pancake House III, version 2b,'" Dwight says. "You'll see the nuance I'm talking about."

Paul clicks on the icon. A short scene from the pancake house plays out on the monitor. The tribe is suddenly back together in their favorite booth:

Duncan and Trent shoot spit wads at each other at each at close range. Trent nails Duncan in the nose with a sticky wad, then Duncan nails Trent in the forehead with a double barrel shot from two straws. Ilima laughs hysterically while Jodi lights a cigarette and leans back and watches the other three with maternal pride. They are happy.

"Hey, no smoking in here!" yells out a voice. Tom, the owner, strides into frame and grabs the cigarette from Jodi's mouth. Duncan starts to rise, but Ilima pulls him back down.

"You punks are in here all the time! This isn't your living room!" He yells at all of them, but he looks straight at Trent. "Don't you have anyplace else to go?"

"No, we don't," Trent says.

"Losers," Tom says.

The tribe falls silent as Tom leaves frame. All happiness is gone. Trent wipes the spit wads from his face and looks out the window. Jodi rubs his back to comfort him while Duncan and Ilima stare at them, wide-eyed and confused.

The scene ends. "Tell me what you see in that scene," Dwight says.

Paul knows he's being set up. No matter what he says, Dwight will find fault with it, but with both the director and the producer present, he must answer.

"I think it's a good scene. The pancake house really was their living room. Trent is clearly the father, trying to provide for his family, and Jodi is the mother hen, making sure everyone is okay. Ilima and Duncan are the two kids just trying to have fun."

"Pretty good," Dwight says, "but you missed something. Tom the owner *also* knows – consciously or subconsciously – that Trent is the father of the group, and he's trying his best to humiliate him in front of his 'children,' played by Duncan and Ilima. That's how strong the family dynamic is. Do you see that now?"

"Yes, now it's clear to me. Thank you, Dwight."

"It's important that you do. This dynamic must be in every scene."

Joel leans forward, clicking and unclicking his watch clasp. "At the same time, Paul, you must always ask yourself, 'what's the story?'"

Paul glances to the left and sees Dwight's leg bouncing. The ticks are back, and both men are once again talking to each other through him. He looks up at the *Junior* poster and into the soft sympathetic eyes of Arnold Schwarzenegger, holding his pregnant belly. He seems to recognize Paul's dilemma, but can do nothing to help.

Dwight taps Paul on the knee to get his attention back.

"The story is our human need to create the family unit, no matter how bad the circumstances are. That's *the* story. That's *their* story. That's *everyone's* story."

"I understand."

"Good. But understanding it is the easy part. Doing it is much harder. The last editor never really got it, which is why I had to take over in the editing chair. But over the next few days we'll see whether you really get it, okay?"

Joel sighs and addresses Dwight directly for the first time. "I'm actually the one hiring him, Dwight. He's on for the full run of the project."

"What if he doesn't get it?"

"Get what? You're the editor, not him. He's here to arrange and organize the two thousand tapes in the next room and find material so you can edit. And no one can find the material faster, because he was there. That's the job."

Dwight laughs and keeps talking to Paul. "We'll give you a two-week grace period and then we'll talk again."

"Paul, I'm the producer and I'm hiring you, not Dwight. I expect you to be at work every day for the next six weeks." Joel stands up. Dwight pushes his chair into the editing position, physically forcing

Paul's chair to the side, with Paul still in it. He starts editing to avoid Joel.

"Gentlemen, this is not a documentary, it's a network made-for-TV movie. It must have a plot laid out in eight acts that are ten to twelve minutes each. The network wants to see a first cut in three weeks. Those are the facts, and they are not going away," Joel says.

He hasn't raised his voice, but Joel's face is so red and bulging that Paul has a vision of Joel falling to the floor with a massive stroke. Dwight keeps staring at the computer screen, using the mouse to drag and drop items between folders. Joel finally leaves.

As the door clicks shut, Dwight speaks. "Everything I've ever done has made it on air. We'll be fine. Go next door and grab me all the tapes from the third week of August."

"Yes sir," Paul answers, and he flips the bird to the back of Dwight's head before he leaves the room.

CHAPTER 22

P aul spends a third of his day working for Dwight, and spends the other two-thirds of his day in the other edit bay on the opposite side of the building. It's the secret room, the shadow room, full of clandestine creativity, and Paul likes it. It is almost a mirror image of the other room. Even the framed posters on the opposing walls seem appropriate to what Paul is doing. On one wall is *The Third Man,* with Orson Welles staring out from the shadows of a doorway in Vienna, and on the opposing side is a different Arnold Schwarzenegger poster, this time as the hunted soldier in the sci-fi action film, *Predator.*

It doesn't take long for Paul to fall into a rhythm, especially since Dwight doesn't want him around anyway. He arrives at 6:30 a.m. and sneaks' tapes from the storage room into the secret bay. He then edits for three solid hours and then sneaks the tapes back into the storage room before Dwight shows up at 10:00 a.m. Paul then works in the storage room organizing tapes and finding shots. But most of the time Dwight ignores him, which gives Paul most of his regular work day to scan tapes and create and revise a plot on paper for Joel's movie.

Paul says "goodnight" to Dwight at 5:00 p.m. and pretends to leave, then sneaks a few more tapes to the secret room and edits his clandestine version of the show until 10:00 p.m. at night, trying out the ideas he'd put to paper during the day. He then goes home and returns at 6:30 a.m. the next day to do it all over again.

Paul soon reduces all that material down to about two hundred interesting moments on tape, and he writes each one down on a different 3x5 card.

Because he rarely gets a request from Dwight, he spends most of his day shuffling through his two hundred cards again and again, laying them out in different patterns, trying to arrange a compelling story. The truth behind the events and the order in which they happened don't matter to him. Their lives are just notes on 3x5 cards now, tiles for the fictional mosaic he is trying to build. Five possible stories emerge, and in each of the five stories, Duncan is the hero.

In real life, Duncan is not a protagonist. He is a lost soul who can't read or write. He is feral, living on instinct, but he appears heroic on TV. He is a near mute in real life, but on screen he is a strong man of few words. He is sometimes obnoxious, rude, and impossible to control, but on screen he is full of youthful rebellion. He has no sense of restraint and will attack people mindlessly until someone pulls him away, which makes him stupid and dangerous. On screen, however, he appears loyal and brave.

Duncan can find fresh food while dumpster diving and senses when danger is coming; however, he can't be trusted with money, making purchases, negotiating with police, or bribing anyone on the street. And the sad truth is that he senses this, but doesn't know how to change his life. That's what Dwight is trying to show in the edit bay on the other side of the building, but Joel and the network won't give him enough time to achieve it, and Joel would never tolerate such a sad but true story anyway.

Paul feels a twinge of guilt for not being a pure filmmaker and pursuing the truth, but he finds a way in his mind to dodge it.

Dwight's pursuit of *the truth* is based on the belief that if you hang around and shoot long enough, people do relax and forget the camera is there. That's what Dwight looks for in *his* edit bay – those brief moments when everyone forgets there's an elephant in the room and people's behavior seems genuine, and he uses those "genuine" moments to build a story.

But Paul can argue there had been no genuine moments at all. Dwight watched everything on a monitor from inside a van, while

Paul had been right there in the room, with a boom in his hand. He'd seen every sidelong glance the kids made to one another while Victor was shooting. He'd seen how the kids would wait for the camera to swing around and rest on a close-up before they spoke.

The kids were homeless, they got hungry, fought, got high and passed out. All that was real. But they also knew they were on TV, and they did their best to give the crew what they thought was a good TV show. They acted.

Paul had heard many off-microphone conversations during which Jodi and Trent argued about whether what the tribe was doing was dramatic enough for the camera. An hour later they'd then complain how the camera cramped their style and how they were being used.

Yet Trent and Jodi never pulled the plug. They saw the production as a path to…what? Fame, celebrity, money, security, who knows? They didn't know either, they just wanted to ride the TV train and see where it went.

At least Jodi and Trent played by the rules and "ignored the camera." Ilima was always a little too thrilled that the production crew was around. She was like an eight-year-old girl at her own birthday party, waving at the camera when the cake shows up and hamming it up as she blew out the candles.

The only person who is oblivious to the camera is Duncan, but not because Duncan is more "real" than the others. Duncan has lived as feral for so long he doesn't understand basic cause and effect. When he sees a suitcase in the train station bathroom he doesn't wonder if it belongs to someone – he just takes it. Ten seconds later when someone attacks him, he doesn't wonder if that person is perhaps the owner of the suitcase – he just fights back. If he can't make the connection between a suitcase and its owner, how can he possibly make the connection between a production crew and a show that is supposed to be on TV months later?

Paul was once an assistant editor on an animal documentary and was amazed at how the production crew and the lions interacted. The production crew would drive straight up next to a pride of lions devouring a zebra and start rolling tape and the lions wouldn't even glance at them. The safari jeeps had been cruising the Serengeti spying on lions for so many generations that the lions now considered them an inconsequential part of the landscape, like an insect or a bird. Second, the lions didn't know or care that they were part of a TV show. That's how Duncan is, and that's why the camera loves him, Paul realizes. He is all instinct, and it reads on screen as charisma, strength, and confidence – so much, in fact, that Paul is confident that Duncan *must* be the hero.

Paul decides to pitch this plot to Joel:

We meet the tribe at the Punk Show out in the Valley, then performing their "skits" on Hollywood Boulevard for money. The audience also sees them in their home downtown in the vats. They are a cohesive family, with Trent as the father/leader and Jodi as his girlfriend/mother, with Ilima as their daughter. Duncan is established as a strong silent outsider who protects the group. He's a streetwise loner who doesn't completely belong, although he wishes he could. He moves in with them.

Duncan entertains them by lighting his hand on fire and parading around the room. The others in the tribe find him delightful. In another scene, the tribe hunts through recycling bins for aluminum cans and glass hoping to make a few dollars to eat, but an evil homeowner wielding a baseball bat attacks them. Luckily, Duncan fights the evil homeowner and saves the day.

The tribe then uses the money they earned from selling the recycling to buy pancakes. We see that despite their poverty they can be happy. It's also clear that Duncan is falling in love with Ilima.

But Ilima is sick and getting sicker. Her cough starts in Act I, but is barely noticeable. As we approach the first hour break she is now hacking up blood.

Trent and Jodi don't have enough money to take her to a private doctor, and they are afraid of hospitals and social workers. If anyone finds out where they live, they could lose their home.

Ilima's health continues to deteriorate, and soon she is trapped in bed with a dangerous fever. The tribe must do something or Ilima may die. The first hour ends with Ilima in bed with the rest of the tribe watching from the next room, worried.

At the start of the second hour, the tribe acts. Jodi sells her gold necklaces to raise money to buy medicine for Ilima – but it's still not enough. Time is running out, so Jodi makes a drastic decision. She decides to prostitute herself on the street to raise the rest of the needed money for Ilima. She bathes, dresses in her most alluring clothes, puts on makeup, and goes out.

She brings a man back to the vats, a young man named Xander, who attacks her. Trent tries to fight back, but Xander overpowers him. Duncan is quick and lethal and easily defeats the evil Xander and saves Jodi.

But Ilima is still sick, and Jodi and Trent have run out of options. Plus, Xander has seen the vats, and may bring others back to take over their home. It's their darkest hour, and there seems to be no way out!

Then Duncan disappears. Trent and Jodi are scared and worried – they need Duncan more than ever, and he's not there to help them.

Then – Duncan returns with a suitcase that is full of clothes that they need, plus – two thousand dollars! "We're rich!" Jodi yells, holding up the wad of money. He doesn't explain where or how he got it, but he has more than enough cash to bring Ilima to the hospital, and to help everyone escape the vats.

They don't want to leave, but they know they have no choice. Trent and Jodi say goodbye to the vats forever, but they swear to Duncan and Ilima that they'll all be together again someday.

Trent and Jodi go, leaving Duncan alone with Ilima. He gathers the sick girl up in his arms and takes her outside and calls 911. The ambulance arrives and the paramedics load Ilima into the ambulance. Duncan takes one last look at the vats and then climbs in with her. The ambulance speeds away.

Paul makes sure the footage from the DV tape he shot is the climax of the show. That tape is finally paying off, but not in the way he expected. He emails the outline to Joel on a Friday night, and Joel phones him in the secret edit room on Saturday morning.

"This is beyond drama, it's melodrama," Joel says. "It's perfect, I love it. Especially the moment when Duncan carries Ilima outside. When did you get that footage?

"I have my ways."

"I'm sure you do. When can I get a first cut?"

CHAPTER 23

Maggie sprawls on the couch and leafs through her Hawaii guidebook. "It says that Kauai is the smallest of the major Hawaiian Islands, but it has the most isolated pristine beaches, more than thirty. Plus, it has a canyon in the middle where the volcano used to be, that is as deep as the Grand Canyon."

"I can hardly wait," Paul says, folding the laundry.

She stretches her arms over her head, arching her back like a cat. "So, when can I buy the tickets?"

Paul looks at the calendar on the refrigerator. It's Sunday, his one day off, and he must deliver a first cut in two weeks. Joel will show it to his network honchos who will give notes, which means a week of changes for Paul. Then he will be done. Online editors and colorists and mixers will finish it the following week, and then it will air.

"The earliest we can get to Hawaii is three weeks from today," Paul says.

"Are you sure? You're already working sixteen hours a day. How do you know he won't extend it?"

"He can't, he's out of money. Plus, there's an air date."

"It's TV. There's always more money, if they like it."

"They won't like it, trust me. At this point, everyone just wants it finished. This is just a bad little made-for-TV movie that will air once and then go away. And then you and I can move on with our lives."

Maggie rolls off the couch and slides into a kitchen chair and watches Paul fold the last of his shirts. "You should've washed the one you're wearing, it's got a stain on it."

"Where?"

"Right there," she answers, and points at his chest. Paul looks down and Maggie flicks her finger up and whacks his nose. "Ha, made you look."

"You're a very clever girl. And very mature."

Maggie steps around the counter into the kitchen. "I feel mature," she says, pushing his laundry aside. "Don't you? I feel for once that I have a bit of control over my life. We're working, we're making money, there's light at the end of the tunnel, we're taking a vacation. Right?" She puts her arms around his neck and tugs his face close to hers and kisses him.

"Yes, you are so very right," he whispers.

"So, you're sure I can buy the tickets and book the hotel?"

"You can buy the tickets and book the hotel. And you and I will sip Mai Tais and make love on some pristine isolated beach."

"Hawaii, here we come."

CHAPTER 24

Paul is worried that the plot he invented is too much of a stretch. The kids really did everything in each of the scenes, so he is confident he has the material. But he is not only changing the order of events, he is also altering the meaning of everything that happened. Would it be believable?

Then, miracle of miracles, he finds a way to make all of it work: reaction shots. With the right kind of reaction shot from one of the kids, he can change the scene into anything he wants. He pastes a shot of a listening tribe member over a shot of another one talking. He can shorten or lengthen what they are saying, and give the other members of the tribe a happy reaction to what's being said. Or angry, or sad, or indifferent.

Since the kids were homeless, they never changed their clothes and they did the same things again and again. It was tedious during production, but it's a gold mine in editing. For this, he has to thank Dwight, the director. Dwight had directed every pancake encounter, for instance, as if it were the turning point of the film. Paul hated him for it in the field, but in the edit bay he is thankful he has so many long lingering shots of each of them staring, laughing, crying, smirking, or saying nothing.

Is Duncan picking his nose or eating his earwax? No problem. Paul just jumps to tapes shot on a different day but in the same location. He looks for some other reaction shot of Duncan, completely out of context – perhaps Duncan looking sick, or looking sad with a knit brow because Trent is yelling at him, or Duncan staring into space. He then steals the shot and drops it into the scene, and it works.

In one scene, Duncan tells a joke in the pancake house that no one thinks is funny, so Paul scours the dozens of other pancake house tapes and finds some other scene where the tribe laughs uproariously for some other reason. Paul cuts it in, and Duncan is funny.

The biggest challenge, however, is finding them saying nice things about one another. For his version, Paul wants them to be a cohesive family, but in the footage, they are often cruel to one another. Paul knows that Dwight is putting all their flaws and warts into his version. You might not know whether you like the kids or hate them when you see his version, which is how Dwight wants it. And that's how it was during production – sometimes you liked the kids and sometimes you just hated them.

But Paul can't leave anything ambiguous. He must make sure the audience is always rooting for the main characters. He scans hundreds of tapes to find Trent and Jodi holding hands, Ilima kissing Duncan on the cheek, Trent slapping Duncan on the back like a good buddy, and the one time every three weeks when they shared a group hug.

The show is coming together. Sure, it looks rough and choppy. The camera shots swing all over the place and the edits are often abrupt and jumpy, but it adds a "documentary" feel that make the false melodrama seem real.

And all the loose ends tighten up when Paul adds music. Dwight never uses music in any of his pieces, except during the opening and closing credits, and it's always classical music. Paul, on the other hand, uses wall-to-wall music to sell his plot. If there's a moment of confusion about what the audience is supposed to feel, Paul hits them over the head with the right music cue: right now, you should feel angry, sad, happy, scared, or inspired. Especially inspired. He puts in soaring music as often as he can, and the kids look as brave and strong and tragic as dying soldiers in World War II, or a tribe of Sioux braves riding their war ponies across the Great Plains.

Exhaustion returns. In production, he had aching thighs and no feeling in his feet and hands. In the edit bay, it's a different kind of tired. His eyes itch and burn, and after hours of sitting, his lower back shoots pain down his hamstrings. He works longer and longer hours, surpassing the sixteen hours a day he did in production, making it to eighteen hours a day, not including his commute.

During his last three days, he never goes home. He works for Dwight during the day, then edits on his own until five a.m., then grabs a few hours of sleep on the couch. At eight a.m., he staggers into the bathroom, splashes water on his face, wipes the smell from under his arms with wet paper towels, then gets a huge dose of coffee.

Once the caffeine smashes into his brain stem, he goes to the other edit bay and powers through two hours of assistant editing work to help Dwight prep for his day. It's interesting to see how different the two shows are. Dwight's version is slowly coming together into a story that is sometimes brilliant but often boring. Yet each day the boring parts get shorter and tighter and eventually disappear. Paul figures that with enough time Dwight would end up with something compelling and original. Maybe that's what Dwight is plotting for – an extension. If Dwight can get something good enough by Friday, Joel may see the light and give him more time. He may have used the same strategy with all his other shows and succeeded. He just doesn't realize yet that Joel has already countered Dwight's secret plan with his own secret plan.

Paul finishes the first cut of his version of the show at three a.m. Friday morning. He blinks at the computer screen, amazed. He leans back and watches the show as the computer lays it down to videotape, but he is too exhausted and too familiar with every edit to know whether it's any good or not. None of the music cues or emotional moments move him at all anymore, and he falls asleep halfway through.

He wakes up during the last five minutes of the show, just as Duncan carries the sick Ilima out of the vats. Duncan stands in the street as the camera sweeps around him, revealing the paramedics racing down the street to rescue the sick girl.

Paul feels a twinge of emotion, but just a tug. It's the same feeling he has at the end of most hour-long TV dramas, just before he switches channels. In other words, it seems like a typical TV show. Paul had succeeded. His version isn't brilliant, it's not original, but it is like everything else on TV, which is exactly what Joel wants.

He feels his exhaustion lift. All he has to do is drop the tape in the outgoing box downstairs for Joel's runner to pick up for home delivery, and he can go home and rest for three days until network notes came back on Monday. But deep down inside, he knows that he has hit the mark and there will be very little for him to do. Paul labels the tape and puts it in a manila envelope, seals it shut, and writes on the outside in black Sharpie pen, "TO: CIA Bureau Chief, Rome. FROM: Field Agent XXX. STATUS: Urgent, Top Priority."

Paul backs up the project, shuts down the computer system, turns out the lights, grabs his jacket, and walks out of the room. It's 4:30 a.m., so most of the building lights are off. The red fire exit signs glowing at the end of the narrow hallways guide him to the front of the building.

Soon he'll be back in bed with Maggie, a full hour before the sun comes up. In two weeks, they'll be in Hawaii and this whole experience will be a distant memory. In four weeks, his life will be his own again. He finds the outgoing runner box at the front desk and drops the tape in.

"What are you doing here?"

Paul whips around. Dwight stands in the shadow of the staircase.

"Dwight, you scared the shit out of me. I didn't know anyone else was here."

"I'm behind on my editing. What's that?" Dwight nods at the manila envelope that Paul just dropped in the outbox.

"It's something I've been working on, on the side."

"At four-thirty in the morning? What is it?"

"It's a music video I've been editing for my friend Andy. It was his gear you wrecked on the shoot. He's tight on money until the insurance company pays off the claim, but he needs this music video finished, so I'm helping him out. I figure I owe him.

Paul amazes himself with that lie, but he can tell Dwight believes him from the way he sighs and hangs his head. "Where are you working?" Dwight asks.

"I made friends with another editor on the other side of the building. He said I could edit my stuff on his system, as long as I did it at night after hours."

"Why didn't you ask me? You don't have to edit on someone else's system in the middle of the night. You can edit on my system any time after eight p.m."

"I knew you were swamped. Plus, I didn't want you to know that I was moonlighting while working on your project. But I guess you caught me."

Dwight steps out of the shadows from under the stairwell. Paul can't help but think that no one would stand there unless they were hiding. Maybe Dwight knew he was coming and was lying in wait.

Dwight pulls out a pack of cigarettes. "I usually don't smoke, but nicotine keeps me awake when I need to pull an all-nighter." He pulls one out and offers the pack to Paul, who takes one. It would keep him awake now, but not smoking with him might be the bigger risk.

"Is that why you're down here? To sneak a cigarette?"

Dwight nods. He pushes open one of the glass doors and lets in a rush of cold autumn air. He kicks off one of his shoes and sticks it in the door to keep it from closing all the way, and gestures for Paul to follow him outside.

Dwight stands there with one shoe on, pulls his leather jacket tight around him and lights his cigarette, then lights Paul's. Dwight breathes deep and exhales blue smoke. Paul takes a light puff.

"Who's in the music video?"

"This new hip hop group that Andy produces. XXX-Tra. You ever heard of them?"

"Nope."

"They're pretty good. I think they're going to make it."

"I'd love to see it. Maybe I could help. Give you some notes."

"That's okay, I know you've got a cut to finish."

"Hey, the whole music video is what? Three minutes, right? I need the break anyway, it'll be a change of pace." Dwight pats Paul on the shoulder, all smiles.

"I told Andy I'd leave it at the front desk for him for early pick-up."

"It's not even 5 a.m. yet. We could play around for three hours before anyone else even shows up, then do another output."

"That's okay, I'm sick of it right now."

"Let me look at it, then. I know a lot of music video production companies. I could put a good word in for you. Get you more directing and editing work."

Paul takes one last drag on his cigarette and drops it. Dwight is calling his bluff and he has just the amount of time it takes to snuff the butt out with his shoe to decide what to do about it.

"That's so cool. Thanks, Dwight. Let me go get the tape."

Paul pulls the door open and walks back inside. For a moment, he considers kicking the shoe out of the door and locking Dwight outside. He could sneak out the back and get the tape to Joel on his own. But then Dwight would know that he's being betrayed. Paul has visions of Dwight kicking in office doors until he finds the secret edit room still full of tapes and destroying the entire computer system and project. Then there would be no show at all, except the one VHS low resolution dub he'd just created.

Paul grabs the envelope from the outbox, steps back outside and hands it to Dwight, who looks at the writing on the outside and laughs.

"CIA Bureau Chief, huh? And I guess you're Agent XXX?"

"We're just kidding around. Andy and I have been obsessed with spy movies ever since we were kids. I'd love to work in that genre."

"That's cool. I know a few people who work on the Bond films. I can pass your name on to them." Dwight says. He turns the package over in his hands, as if he were trying to see through the envelope.

"I'm exhausted, I have to go. I want to get a few hours of sleep before I come back in," Paul yawns. "Can you tell me what you think of it when I see you again at ten? I'd be in better shape to absorb your notes."

"You don't have to come back in, take the day off," Dwight declares.

"What about your cut? It's due today. Don't you need help with the output?"

"I can handle it myself. You've been working hard."

"Will I still get paid? Sorry to ask," Paul says.

"I'll make sure of it."

"Can I call you in the edit bay at 10 to get your notes then?"

"Sleep in, I'll watch it and then call you."

"I'd love to hear what you think about the speed of the edits. I edited out of step with the music. I'm a drummer and I picked a 5/4 pace for the edit, so I'm behind the beat, then I catch up, and then pass it, and then it catches up to me. I think it's cool, so I hope you like it."

"I'll keep my eye out for that," Dwight says, holding up the package. Paul can tell that Dwight is tired of talking to him.

"Thanks, Dwight." Paul smiles and starts walking away. He stops and turns back. "Oh, can you do me a favor?"

"Sure, what's up?"

"After you look at the video would you put it back in the envelope, tape it up and leave it downstairs for me again? I think there's packing tape in the drawers behind the receptionist's desk. That way Andy's runner can still pick it up on time and I can do your notes on the next pass."

Dwight holds the envelope up. "No problem. I'll do it right after I watch it."

"Thanks Dwight. And thanks for passing my name on to the music video production companies and the Bond people. I really appreciate it."

"Don't mention it."

Paul waves an awkward goodbye, then keeps walking. He rounds the corner of the building and stops. He exhales slowly. When he hears the glass front doors of the building close, he leans down and peeks back around the edge of the building. Dwight is back inside the closed glass lobby. He watches Dwight walk over to the outgoing box and drop the manila envelope back inside without ever opening the package.

As Paul watches Dwight walk back up the stairs toward his edit bay, Paul hopes he'll never see Dwight again.

CHAPTER 25

P aul arrives at Maggie's front door at the same time as the morning paper. In fact, Paul must wait while the paper boy in the pickup makes six tosses through his passenger side window, one for each resident who pays for the paper, nailing the front gate each time. He tosses the last one to Paul and then drives away.

Paul is wide awake after that cigarette and even more pumped after the close call with Dwight, but he still takes off his clothes and crawls into bed with Maggie. It's 5:45 a.m. He spoons her from behind and she sighs and turns to meet him. Her eyes widen.

"You stink. Yuck."

"I do?"

"Like cigarettes and body odor and bad Indian food."

"I've been working three days straight."

"Get out! These sheets are clean, and I don't want you in here, you animal." She pushes him away with her hands and feet. Paul reaches under the covers and touches her bare legs with his cold hands, making her jump.

"Stop it, Icicle Man! I can sleep for another hour, leave me alone."

Paul climbs out of bed. He puts on a robe, goes into the kitchen, puts on coffee and leafs through the pile of mail waiting for him on the counter. There are two paychecks, six bills, his bank statement, and plane tickets. He opens the envelope with the tickets and reads the itinerary – flight to Honolulu, another flight to Maui, free shuttle to the hotel, and twelve nights and thirteen days at the Kaanapali Beach Hotel. *Didn't she say Kauai?* He's sure she did but decides to roll with it. Paul stares at the plane ticket. He is thirty-one years old, and this is the first time seeing his name on a plane ticket for a vacation that he bought for himself.

Maggie bought it though. *Time to fix that.* He grabs his checkbook and calculator from the side table, pours himself coffee, and opens envelopes. Once he deposits his two paychecks, his bank account will be in full bloom, but then he must deal with his Visa bill, his student loan (still in arrears), his share of the rent and utilities, the money he owes the film lab where his film is locked up, his car payments, and now this vacation.

When he finishes his calculations he almost throws his coffee cup through the kitchen window. He doesn't have enough to pay her for the trip, even with one more paycheck coming. One of the bills will have to go unpaid, but which one?

He glances out the window. He hasn't seen the repo guys in three weeks. He sent in five months of payments, but he is still behind on four. He should pay that bill off first. But then his girlfriend would pay for their entire trip to Hawaii.

Paul decides to gamble. He writes three checks and empties his bank account. His Visa balance is low enough that creditors won't call, he is up to date on his student loans, and the biggest check goes to Maggie for the rent and the vacation. His last paycheck will cover next month's bills but then he'll be broke again, with four back payments still due on that damn car, which he hasn't driven in months. And his film? He feels like he'll never get it out of the lab.

But he'll worry about that next month, when he gets back from vacation, tanned and rested. It will be a new chapter in his life. This trip will be good. He is giving himself a real vacation in a real hotel, like an adult. He and Maggie will finally patch things up. Her place is feeling more and more like his place, too.

He hears a car outside and peeks out the window. The brown Oldsmobile Cutlass slowly drives by.

CHAPTER 26

The phone rings Monday morning. It's Joel with the network notes.

"Are you sitting down?"

"Just give me the notes, Joel," Paul answers.

"They like the show. They want to air it in two weeks."

"You're kidding me."

"They didn't pee their pants with excitement, just to be clear. Mostly they're relieved, especially after watching Dwight's versions of the show for the past month."

Paul feels torn; part of him hoped they'd be gushing, but it's also the reaction he expected. They'll air the show, people will see it, and the next week some other show will slide into its place, and this project will be lost forever in the vast endless media river.

Then Paul gets scared. What he really needs right now is a paycheck for one more week. If they like the show and there are no big changes, he just worked himself out of a job, and there will be no money to pay next month's bills. He'd done an entire budget based on getting one more week of work out of it.

"That's it? There are no notes?"

"Just one note, and it's big," Joel says. "Right now, the show ends with Duncan carrying Ilima outside, he calls 911, the ambulance arrives and he and Ilima ride away together. Brilliant. I don't know why the hell Dwight never put it in his versions but forget him. Now the executives want to end the show in the hospital room and show that she's okay, with all the other three kids surrounding her."

"We can't do that."

"Why not? It's just one note." He sounds irritated, as if Paul is being difficult.

"Because we don't have that footage. We didn't shoot it."

"You didn't shoot it? Why didn't you shoot it? It's so clear the story needs it!" Joel shouts. "I can't believe you blew this!"

Paul takes the phone from his ear and stares at it. It's a surreal joke. Has Joel completely forgotten what kind of show he is producing?

Paul wants to scream into the phone that the whole show is a fake, that Paul had invented this whole story in the edit bay, and that he is the one who rescued the show from documentary oblivion and turned it into a reality movie against all odds. And now Joel is trying to turn it all around and pretend that the *one problem* with the show is somehow Paul's fault? As if they were doing an episode of *Law and Order* and Paul had neglected to shoot the final scene written in the script?

Paul almost yells into the phone, but then he remembers the final paycheck he needs, plus the vacation, and his car, locked in the garage outside, that the repo men still want. He must play this just right.

"Ask Dwight to do it, I'm just the assistant editor on this," Paul says, and hangs up. Paul pours himself a glass of water and waits. Ten minutes go by and the phone rings. Paul lets the machine pick up. It's Joel.

"Okay, okay, you proved your point. Please pick up the phone. Hello? Paul? Hello? Can you please pick up the phone?"

Paul picks up. "I'm listening."

"I need your help, okay? I admit it. Please Paul, we are so close to finishing."

"What do you mean, 'we?'" Paul asks. "You're the producer, Dwight's the director, I'm just the guy behind the curtain working my ass off. And I've done the job you hired me to do. There's nothing else in this for me."

"Paul, it's just one note."

"We didn't shoot it! It didn't happen!"

"And I explained that to them, but the network doesn't care. They don't care that this is a 'documentary reality' show, they're too busy to care how this process works, and they don't care how hard we've been working. They just want this show to look like a regular made-for-TV movie. That's all they care about."

Paul tries to imagine these network executives. Who were they? Did they all watch it together, and talk about it? No, they probably each watched it alone in their different offices while answering phones and skimming the trade publications. Then they all traded emails and moved to the next show in the pile on their desk. Asking Joel to make a change to a TV show is like asking a secretary to change the last paragraph in a multi-page memo. They just give the note and expect it to be done.

"We got *one* note. Trust me, we got off easy."

Paul searches through his memory, scanning all his mental cubby holes for any shots that might do the trick. He finds nothing.

"Do a write-on. Just fade out and put white letters over black, saying that Ilima was taken to the hospital, got better, and they all lived happily ever after."

"I tried that. They want one more scene."

"There's nothing else!"

"Not if we shoot a new ending. You could direct it."

The words hang in the air. He thinks of Dwight, toiling away in his edit bay, hating both Paul and Joel and insisting on staying true to his work, refusing to submit to the network executives sitting behind their desks piled high with papers and tapes, unaware of this subterfuge. Paul admires Dwight's tenacity, even if he is a jerk. Part of Paul's brain wants to say "no" to Joel; shooting a new final scene for someone else's work is going too far. Then again, Paul knows that Dwight doesn't care one iota about him, and would gladly screw him over if it serves him.

"Paul?" Joel asks. "Are you still there?"

Paul looks up and sees the calendar on the wall, with a big X on this coming Sunday, his vacation, just a week away. He glances into the bedroom and sees Maggie's open suitcase on the bed surrounded by the clothes that she'd been packing and unpacking in different combinations all weekend in excited anticipation. This vacation must happen, no matter what.

"I'll do it."

"Good. You're a smart man."

"But I need a couple of things."

"You name it."

"I don't want to edit anymore. I don't want to even walk in that building."

"No problem. The publicity department wants to start making promos. I'll get one of their editors to edit the last scene and finish the show."

"And I want a real producer helping me organize everything. We have to find Duncan and Ilima again, I need a real crew, we have to find a hospital–"

"That goes without saying. The network has already approved those overages."

"And I don't want any editing credit or directing credit of any kind. I just want the sound mixer credit," Paul says.

"Are you sure about that?"

"Completely. I don't want Dwight to come after me with a gun."

"That's a bit of an exaggeration, but okay."

"And we have to shoot this by Friday. I'm going on vacation Sunday."

"That's a little tight. But if you find the kids in time, no problem."

"And I want five thousand dollars in cash, up front."

Now it's Joel's turn to pause. Paul hangs on the line, listening to him slowly exhale. He waits, wondering if he asked for too much.

"Three thousand. Cash makes it tough."

"Thirty-five hundred then. And fifteen hundred in a check after it airs."

"Deal."

"I better get busy. The line producer can call me this afternoon," Paul says, and hangs up. $3500 will pay off his car completely, lower his Visa bill, and get his film out of the lab, and he'll come home to another $1500 check, which he can give to Maggie for future rent. And he'll own that car outright. That's more of a future than he's ever had as an adult. Life is getting better.

He looks at his watch. It's eleven a.m. on Monday. The last possible safe day they can shoot this is Friday, which would give them one extra day if something goes wrong (and it always does) which would push the shoot into Saturday. That gives him three days to somehow find the kids. Duncan will be the hardest.

CHAPTER 27

F inding Ilima is easy. The new line producer, Kevin, tracks her down in Orange County living with cousins, babysitting during the day and working as a Baskin Robbins ice cream scooper in the evening. Trent and Jodi turn up in a residence hotel in the bowels of Hollywood. They work as bar-backs and janitors at two clubs on Santa Monica Boulevard, Club Focker and The Extreme Dream.

Now Joel must convince the tribe to let cameras back into their lives while Paul's job is to find Duncan and make sure the shoot happens before Saturday. Joel gives Paul a Ford Escort rental car to search Los Angeles, along with a company cell phone so that Joel and Kevin can call him every hour with questions and progress reports on the upcoming shoot day.

Paul starts his search for Duncan at the vats and finds twenty homeless men living there. They throw glass bottles at him and chase him out of the building.

Paul gets another call from Joel. Ilima, Trent and Jodi are happy to have the cameras back in their lives again, but they are savvy enough to know that they don't have to do anything for free anymore. Ilima's cousin, a big Hawaiian guy named Kai, acts as her agent and says that Ilima will do it for three thousand, and Joel must pay for Ilima's dental work. That's easy enough – Joel puts her on the network payroll, gets her medical and dental insurance, and lines her up with a Century City dentist who will fill all her cavities.

Paul looks through all the homeless shelters and shows everyone a photo of Duncan taken from the footage. Street people, Catholic nuns, and counselors all shake their heads. No one knows him or has seen him.

Paul worries that someone will ask him why he's searching for him. What is he supposed to answer? "I'm doing a TV movie and we need him for a shoot on Friday?" But no one asks; everyone assumes he is either a private eye or a social worker.

Paul searches for Duncan in Union Station when Kevin calls for the tenth time. Trent and Jodi finally agree to do the shoot, but they want more than Ilima does. Trent and Jodi want free rent for a year in a one-bedroom apartment in a secure building on Franklin Avenue. Joel negotiates them down to six months and insists that his name be on the rental agreement, so he can kick them out if there is any trouble. He also insists that the final scene be shot there, so he can write the apartment off as a production location. Paul then sits down in Union Station and strategizes with Kevin over the phone about what props they'll need to transform a one-bedroom apartment into a passable hospital room.

Paul then searches Hollywood Boulevard back alleys, bars, and all the nightclubs. Paul felt a certain kinship with Duncan during shooting, an unspoken connection that Paul believes will now somehow help him find the feral boy. But by 2 a.m. on Thursday, Paul suggests they hire a private detective to help track him down. Joel refuses.

"I'm already paying you five thousand. You can find him," Joel says over the phone.

On Thursday, Paul scours downtown and all the city parks where homeless people squat, with no luck. On Thursday night, Paul tries the nightclubs next, but people want to dance and drink and pick each other up. They aren't interested in looking at Duncan's photo and answering Paul's questions. Paul gives up at 4:30 a.m. Friday morning and goes home to eat, shower, and change his clothes.

He needs rest, but if he lies down now he will sleep for twelve hours, which he can't afford. Instead, he writes checks while eating cereal. The $3500 from Joel went into his bank account yesterday.

Paul leaves a check for Maggie on the desk, then seals and stamps the envelope that holds the check for all his remaining car payments. He stares at it, amazed. One trip to the post office and that hassle will be over. In a few days he'll be on vacation, and he'll return to $1500 more in the bank, no repo men chasing him, and a new life with Maggie. But he has to find Duncan.

He showers, and then tries to be quiet while digging through the closet.

Maggie wakes up and rolls over in bed. "How's it going?"

"Not good." He finds a dark blazer and puts it over a clean white shirt.

"I haven't seen you in four days. We're still going to Hawaii, right?"

Paul crawls onto the bed in the dark, pinning her underneath the covers, tucking her in on all sides with the comforter.

"I will be here on Sunday morning at six a.m. with my bags packed, waiting for the shuttle with you, whether this show is finished or not," Paul says. He stands up and opens his arms. "These are the only clean clothes I have left. How do I look?"

"Like a cop."

"Good. That might help," he says. He pecks her cheek and leaves again.

Paul drives his rented Ford Fiesta to the post office and drops his envelope through the mail slot, which makes him feel ten pounds lighter. The he drives down to the Hillbilly Girl pancake house, but the owner says he hasn't seen Duncan in weeks. Paul is now too sleep-deprived to keep driving and goes back to Maggie's to sleep for a few hours. He calls Kevin from the car and pushes the shoot to Saturday morning.

Paul sets three alarms and pushes Maggie's open suitcase to the corner of the bed and falls face first into the pillow. He has another eight hours to find Duncan, otherwise he'll have to design over-the-shoulder shots with a lookalike stand-in, or maybe he can cheat an extreme close-up of Duncan from some other tape…and he drifts off to sleep.

The alarms go off a second later, it seems. Paul puts on his jacket, darts out of the apartment, bounds down the stairs – and spots the brown Cutlass parked just outside the gate. Paul does a cartoon stop and darts back behind the wall before they spot him.

Damn, this is bad timing. The car is paid in full, postmarked today, but they're never going to believe his check is in the mail, and with only eight hours to find Duncan, he doesn't have time to argue with them. He must dodge them until the finance company gets his check, then the whole nightmare will be over.

Paul crosses the courtyard, opens a door and goes downstairs into the building's basement and into the laundry room. An older lady from the back apartment, Sarah, folds hot towels coming out of the dryer. Paul stands on a stepladder and opens the steel grating that covers a basement window.

"If you leave that open, thieves will get in," Sarah says.

"I was hoping you could close it for me after I crawl out," Paul says.

"You're nothing but trouble. I told Maggie that she could do a lot better than you."

"You're probably right. Will you close the window after I squeeze out?"

Paul jumps up and squeezes his upper torso through the basement window.

Sarah keeps right on talking. "She's better off with that handsome British boy, Rupert. He treats her much better than you do."

Paul pauses with his body halfway through the window, wondering what Sarah knows. The lawn sprinklers go off, soaking him. Paul squeezes the rest of the way through, streaking his dress pants and blazer with grass and mud.

Rupert? He hasn't seen that pompous British prick for weeks, he's supposed to be in the Caribbean on some movie shoot, playing another pirate. Did something happen between Maggie and Rupert? Paul pushes his anger back down. He's sure Rupert hit on Maggie, but there's no proof that she took him up on his offer. Even if she did, Paul can't fault her, knowing what he's put her through in the past six months. All he can do now is keep every promise to her, make her proud, and win her back.

Paul darts down the back alley past two buildings before heading back to the street. He parked his rental car a few doors down from Maggie's building just in case this happened. The repo men are still in front of Maggie's building, a hundred yards away.

He creeps up to the Ford Escort from the street side, opens the door and gets behind the wheel without being noticed, but when he starts the engine, both repo men turn. The Enforcer starts lumbering down the street towards him. The Escort is stuck between two parked cars and Paul twists the wheel as hard as he can. The Enforcer is almost there. Paul hits the "lock" button and seals all the doors.

A hand touches Paul's shoulder. He screams and spins around and sees Duncan lying down in the back seat.

"What are you doing there?" Paul screams.

Duncan grins. "I heard you were looking for me."

"I am. We need you for some more shooting for the TV show."

"Okay. That's cool."

The Enforcer yanks on the driver's side door then pounds on the glass.

"I paid everything! The check for the rest is in the mail!"

"It's too late for that, we want the car back!" the Enforcer screams. He keeps pounding on the glass, trying to break it. The glass cracks. Paul looks at Duncan, still grinning in the back seat.

"Can you make these guys go away?"

Duncan opens the passenger door and jumps out just as the Businessman swings a punch at him. Duncan ducks it, kicks him in the stomach, pulls his leather jacket over his head, and pushes him down between two parked cars. The Enforcer steps around the car and swings his fist at Duncan, who easily dodges the punch and kicks the big man in the balls. The Enforcer gasps and falls to his knees, holding his crotch. Paul nudges the Escort's front bumper out in the street, Duncan jumps in, and they drive off.

Paul glances in the rearview mirror to see if the repo men are following him, then laughs out loud. Duncan sees Paul laughing, so he laughs too.

"Where have you been for the last two months?" Paul asks.

"Around. I've been living in a school bus."

"Well maybe we can change that. How does that sound?"

"Whatever. Can you buy me lunch?"

"Hang on a second," Paul says. He grabs his cell phone and hits the redial button.

Kevin answers on the other end. "Did you find him?"

"Yes. How soon can I shoot?"

"In thirty minutes."

"We're on our way. Can you order lunch for us?"

"Food will be waiting by the time you get here. There's a guard holding a parking spot for you out front. The set decorator is on her way."

Paul hangs up, impressed by Kevin. Maybe he'll get a chance to work with more people like Kevin in the future.

Thirty minutes later, Duncan wolfs down a hamburger while Paul checks out what will soon be Trent and Jodi's new apartment. It's a small one-bedroom with an ugly chocolate marble rug, and a view of the Hollywood freeway.

"I don't see how this is going to work as a hospital room."

"Tell you what, Mr. Director. You do your job and I'll do mine, okay?" Kevin says. "Trust me, you won't even recognize this place."

Workmen arrive with the discarded hospital set from the network soap opera *Malibu Promises*. When Kevin and Joel heard the show was getting a production upgrade, they "bought" the old set from the studio lot. A dozen people move in a hospital bed, machines, lamps, and plants. They hang vertical curtains and fake art work. They hammer bookcases into the walls, and wheel in a big green oxygen tank with a mask and medical tubing. Gaffers hang fluorescent hospital lights from the ceiling.

Watching it all happen, Paul feels something that he has never felt before – the invisible support of a TV network that wants its show done on time. There is nothing special or personal about the support, however; in fact, Paul feels almost superfluous as the workers flow in and out of the apartment. Kevin controls the show, yelling, pointing, and barking into his cell phone while madness whirls around him. Paul's little shoot is just one of Kevin's jobs this week.

A woman offers Paul a clean shirt. She takes his dirty blazer and shirt to be dry-cleaned and hands him a moist rag to wipe the mud off his dress pants.

A craft service zone appears in the kitchen, with tables and counters covered with every conceivable fruit and snack, with foods for carnivores, vegetarians or vegans. Duncan sits himself down in the kitchen and devours fistfuls of candy, beef jerky, and apples, and washes it all down with a tall bottle of Pellegrino sparkling water.

Jodi and Trent walk in wearing huge grins. "Is this our new place?" Jodi asks. They spot Duncan and they all run into each other's arms for a group hug, jumping up and down, screaming.

Trent sees Paul and sticks out his hand. Paul smiles and offers his, and Trent pulls him in for a big bear hug. Jodi punches him in the arm.

"Dog, it's so good to see you," Trent says. "I didn't think I'd miss you guys, hassling us with your microphones and batteries and cameras, but I do, I really do."

"I missed you guys too."

"Where's Dwight? And crazy Victor?" Jodi asks.

"That's a long story." Trent and Jodi look confused. Kevin steps in and interrupts before they can ask anything more.

"Jodi? Trent? Hello, I'm Kevin, your line producer," he says, shaking each of their hands. "We need you in makeup right now in the hallway. Paul? The gaffer tells me they'll be ready to shoot in half an hour."

"What about Ilima?" Paul asks.

Kevin's clicks his walkie-talkie. "This is Kevin on set. Can I get an ETA on Ilima please?" He listens patiently to the buzz in his headset and turns to Paul.

"She's getting into the limo now. She came out of anesthesia about an hour ago."

"Anesthesia?"

"She just had all her fillings done and her wisdom teeth pulled. Joel thought it would add to the effect you wanted."

Thirty minutes later Ilima arrives. Fifteen people pause and watch as her cousin Kai and her limo driver lead her across the room and help her crawl into bed. Her eyes are red, and her cheeks are so swollen, she looks like a chipmunk who's been mugged. She pulls up the covers and smiles and waves, and the whole room applauds. The makeup woman sidles up to Paul.

"There's nothing for me to do, I think she looks great," she whispers.

Paul looks around – the only thing missing now is the camera crew. Right on cue, two men walk through the doorway and nod to Kevin, who starts yelling.

"Camera and Audio are here! If you're not camera, audio, lighting, the director, or a cast member, please clear the set and go outside! Thank you!" he yells, and then looks at Paul. "I'm also an assistant director. Just got my union card."

The cameraman and the audio mixer are sturdy men who look like Special Forces soldiers. The cameraman pushes through the departing crowd and shakes Paul's hand.

"Sorry we're late. I'm Mike Lewis, this is my sound mixer, Sandy Cramer."

"I'm Paul Franti. Where are you guys coming from?"

"Belize. We just finished shooting the third season of *Paradise Games* and the network and Joel flew us back early for this. Where do you want the camera?"

Paul looks around the room. Ilima is in bed asleep with puffy cheeks. Trent and Jodi sip coffee next to the bed and stare at him with suspicious eyes. The gaffer, some bald guy he hasn't even spoken to, keeps changing light bulbs. Duncan is back in the kitchen eating more food. Paul points to the foot of the bed.

"We'll start here. The whole show is hand-held, so we don't need any sticks. We'll start on Ilima's face, then pull out to reveal that Duncan is in the chair next to her. Then we'll pan over and pick up Trent and Jodi as they walk in the door. Then just cover the scene as it plays."

"What about audio?" Sandy asks.

"You can boom it, but put radio mics on Trent and Jodi."

While Mike sets up the camera and Sandy preps the microphones for Trent and Jodi, Paul tries to prepare Duncan. Paul motions for him to put down the beef jerky.

"Duncan? This is just like we did before, when you carried Ilima to the ambulance. All you do is look at Ilima and hold her hand. Okay?"

"Just like before. And if Ilima wants to hold hands, I hold hands," he says.

Paul tugs him to his feet, pulls him into the fake hospital room and puts him in the chair next to the bed. Paul taps on Ilima's arm and wakes her up. She smiles.

"Ilima, we're ready to start shooting. You close your eyes, and when you hear me say 'action,' you open your eyes and look at Duncan and smile, just like you're smiling at me now. Okay?"

Ilima nods and closes her eyes again. Jodi and Trent look at him and shrug.

"What do we do?"

"Just stand in the doorway. When I point at you, just walk up to the bed."

"And that's it?" Jodi asks. "We don't say anything?"

"If you want to say something, tell Ilima that the doctor told you she's going to be all right."

Paul gets into position in the corner of the room. Mike and Sandy nod. Duncan stares out the window into space.

"Roll tape."

"We have speed," Mike says.

"Action."

Ilima opens her eyes. She sees Duncan and smiles. He smiles back. She reaches out and touches his hand. He takes it. Mike moves in and gets two-shots and single shots of each of them, then a cutaway shot of them holding hands. Paul points to Trent and Jodi in the doorway. They walk in slowly and go to the other side of the bed.

"The doctors said you're going to be okay," Trent says.

Ilima smiles. She looks at Trent and Jodi and nods her thanks. She reaches out with her left hand to Duncan and with her right hand to Trent. All four tribe members form a circle and hold hands. Mike moves around the circle, still shooting.

"Okay – cut, but no one move," Paul says, "just hold hands and keep looking at one another." The tribe freezes, all still holding hands. Mike glances at Paul, ready for whatever is next.

"Give me long singles on each of their faces, and then drop back for a wide shot of the whole room with them in the middle," Paul says.

Mike nods and keeps rolling, catching smiles, glances, and empty blank faces. Then he drops back, stands on a chair and gets the whole group in a wide shot.

"Cut. We're done."

Kevin walks back in the room. "That's a wrap folks, we need all this furniture broken down and out on the truck in thirty minutes!"

"Can't we keep it?" Jodi asks.

Joel Cuvney walks into the room. He must have arrived in the middle of shooting. "You want your living room to look like this?" he asks Jodi. "With a hospital bed in it?"

"It's the only furniture we have," she says.

"Fine. Keep everything."

"Who are you?" Jodi asks.

"I'm the guy who signed the lease for you, so be good," he says to her. He has no desire to meet her or know her. She's just a cast member who wants something. He turns to the shooter. "Mike, I need that videotape."

Mike ejects the tape and hands it to Joel, who slides it into his bag. Joel turns to Paul. "It's been a pleasure doing business with you, sir." Joel offers his hand and they shake. "Enjoy your vacation. A check for fifteen hundred dollars will be waiting for you when you get back. We'll be in touch," he says, then leaves.

Kai comes back in and helps a groggy Ilima out of bed and out the door. Mike and Sandy pack up and leave next, the gaffer takes down his lights, the craft service evaporates from the kitchen, and the makeup chairs disappear from the hallway. Paul notices that Duncan is gone too. He's like a cat; if you leave the front door open, he'll sneak outside and disappear. Soon it's just Trent and Jodi standing in their new living room, an exact replica of the hospital room on *Malibu Promises*.

"That was weird," Paul says.

"Weird and unreal," Trent says. "But cool. Thanks, Paul."

"When's this thing going to be on TV?" Jodi asks, as she throws herself on her new hospital bed.

"Sometime in the next two weeks. There will even be commercials. Call Joel, he'll tell you.

"Who's Joel?" Trent asks.

Kevin sticks his head back in. "Paul, you can leave the keys to your rental car with me. A production assistant will drive you back home."

Paul realizes it's over. He looks at his watch. It's six p.m. In twelve hours, he and Maggie will be sitting in an early shuttle on the way to the airport.

We'll probably never see you again, huh Paul?" Trent says.

"You never know."

"But probably not," Jodi says.

"Like I said, you never know. Thanks guys. It's been real."

They laugh as Paul walks out. A production van is parked in front with its doors open, waiting for Paul. The woman who offered him the clean shirt now stands holding Paul's dry-cleaned shirt and blazer. He changes into his clothes while standing in the street, then climbs in the van. They pull away.

At the stop light at the end of the street, Paul spots Duncan sitting on a bench at the bus stop. He rolls down his window.

"I was looking for you. Why did you leave?"

"I was bored. I have to be somewhere," Duncan says.

"Don't you want to hang out with Trent and Jodi?"

"They don't want me around anymore. I'm going back to the school bus."

"Do you want a ride?" Paul asks. Duncan shakes his head. The streetlights change and the cars behind them start honking. Paul motions for the production assistant to pull over into the bus stop.

Paul digs through his wallet and pulls out forty dollars and hands it through the window to Duncan. "Take this. And you know where I live, right?"

Duncan nods. He jams the cash into his front pocket like it's tissue.

"If you get into trouble, you come find me, okay?" Paul says

Duncan points to the scar on the side of his head, and then points to the scar on the back of Paul's head, and smiles. Full circle. The car pulls away.

"That guy's weird," the production assistant driver says. "I can't believe you guys did a TV show about him."

"Neither can I." Paul wonders if Duncan even understands that the show is going to air soon. He can't help thinking that Duncan won't live very long.

The production assistant drops Paul off at the front gate of Maggie's building then speeds away. Paul is about to let himself through the front gate when he hears hammering from the side driveway of the building.

Paul peeks around the corner just in time to see the Businessman smashing off the lock and lifting the door to Maggie's garage. The Businessman gets behind the wheel of Paul's Toyota Corolla, and starts it with a magical pass key and backs it down the driveway of the apartment building. He sees Paul standing on the curb and slows down just long enough to flip him off before driving away.

"Shit," Paul says. That was twenty-four thousand dollars, gone forever.

He hears a noise and spins on his heel. The Enforcer punches Paul in the nose. Paul falls to his knees and holds his hands up to catch the blood gushing from his nostrils. He stays down on the cement until he hears the brown Cutlass driving away.

CHAPTER 28

P aul has a few short vivid memories of the next thirty-six hours, all of them cinematic enough to be worthy of inclusion in his mental movie file. He remembers getting to his feet and staggering to the front gate, struggling to get his key in the front lock, then closing his eyes and falling. He remembers Sarah, the old lady from the back apartment, kicking him as she got her mail from the mailbox.

"Get up! You're staining the sidewalk!" she hissed.

Paul remembers someone carrying him, then opening his eyes and seeing Rupert's face staring down at him. That bugged him, that Rupert could carry him so easily, like he's some doll. Wasn't he supposed to be out of town?

He remembers Maggie driving him in her car and glancing down and seeing that the front seat was covered with towels to catch his blood. He remembers waking up in the hospital emergency room and seeing Maggie arguing with a nurse. He heard wheezing, then glanced to his left and saw a man with a kitchen knife sticking out of his chest, and each time he breathed his chest whistled like a kid's toy. He remembers a doctor grabbing his nose between his hands and pushing the broken bone back into place with a click, which sent white lightning bolts of pain shooting through his skull right to his brain stem. He screamed. Paul hallucinated that he was lying on the cement out in front of the Chinese Theater again. Hands stuck wads of cotton up his nostrils, then glued his nose into place with what felt like duct tape.

"Open your mouth," he hears Maggie say, and she drops in a pill, followed by a straw. Paul sips and closes his eyes and lets the black curtains in his head close completely. The curtains part just four more times, for brief but vivid moments.

"Paul!" he hears Maggie yell. He opens his eyes and sees that he is on the couch in the apartment. She holds up some ugly plaid surfer shorts that he doesn't remember owning. "Lift your legs, I'm dressing you!" He glances down and sees he's in just his underwear. Maggie yanks the shorts up his legs and he lifts his ass off the couch enough for her to pull them the rest of the way up to his waist.

He wakes up in a shuttle van full of people speeding through the blue pre-dawn light. He can't stop shivering, and then realizes that he is dressed in beach clothes while everyone else in the van is wearing autumn coats. Maggie sits next to him with her jaw set, staring straight ahead with laser-like focus.

"I'm cold."

"You'll live."

He drifts away again.

"Is he fit to fly?" someone asks next. Maggie props him against the plastic wall of the jet way ramp leading down to the plane door and leans against him to keep him from falling over. Maggie pulls out a white piece of paper and shows the stewardess, who stares into Paul's eyes as if looking for life. He smiles and flashes a "thumbs up" at her just before the black curtains close again.

"Yuck, he's drooling on me," someone says, and Paul feels an elbow jab him in the ribs. He wakes up on a 767 jet in the center row of chairs, leaning over a teenage girl with dreadlocks and a pierced eyebrow.

Maggie tugs him upright and wipes his mouth. "Brace up, we're almost there."

How is Maggie doing this? Does she have super powers? he wonders, and the black curtains fall again for many hours.

Paul wakes up in blackness. The only light is the green glow from the radium on his wristwatch, which says one o'clock. He stretches and feels crisp white sheets around him. He touches them tentatively, worried that he'll find moist stickiness from yet some other gooey accident, but all is fine. A low and thin horizontal line of light appears at one end of the room. Paul eases out of bed and moves towards the line. It's daylight seeping through the base of the curtains. His outstretched hands finally touch fabric and he pulls them open.

The room fills with light. Palm trees and a white sandy beach stretch out below, while some other island floats in the blue ocean on the horizon. A catamaran loaded with people coasts up to the beach. Light and dark bodies dot bright towels on the sand and around the pool below. He made it. He is in Hawaii.

He looks at the room. It's big, with a king-size bed, a sofa, two chairs, and an enormous TV. Maggie's side of the bed is messy, which reassures Paul that they are, in fact, still sharing a room. He wanders into the bathroom, turns on the light and blinks when he sees his reflection in the mirror. He has two black eyes and a swollen red nose covered with a broad strip of surgical tape. His skin is so white against the black marble that he seems to glow like an alien. He hears the door open. Paul grabs a white robe from the hook before stepping back into the room.

"Look who's back from the dead," Maggie says. She wears a yellow bikini with a blue silk pareo around her hips, sandals, and a broad beach hat. She takes off her sunglasses, throws her beach bag on the bed, and plops into a chair. She looks like she's been living in Hawaii for months. Paul smells coconut oil coming from her smooth skin. She stares at him with no emotion on her face.

"Is this Kauai?" Paul asks.

"Maui. Kaanapali Beach. I changed our plans two weeks ago. I told you that."

"I look like shit."

"You sure do. And I worked my ass off getting you here."

"I appreciate it." Paul leans over and kisses her. She meets his lips and kisses him back, which is a good sign. The leaning makes his head throb, but he doesn't dare wince. Paul eases down in the chair opposite her.

"How's the pain?"

"It's a dull throb. It's not that bad. I guess he broke my nose."

"You got that right. And I had to pay for the emergency room with my credit card, which came to $1500. Plus, those repo guys broke the garage door to get your car, which my landlord is going to love."

"They can't do that. And they can't just hit me. I paid everything I owed so far on that car, too. We've got a lawsuit if we want one."

"All I want right now is a vacation, so I'm only going to ask this once. Are we on vacation or not?"

Paul lifts his left hand and put his right hand over his heart. "I will not mention work or Joel or lawsuits or moan about my injuries for two whole weeks. I will swim and snorkel and sail and surf and not complain once. I swear."

Maggie pulls him by the hands across the room, opens his robe and pushes him back on the bed. Paul's skull aches when it hits the pillow, but he remembers his promise and keeps his mouth shut. Maggie runs her hands across his chest.

"You need some color, Phosphorescent Man," she whispers as she straddles him.

He reaches up and pops her breasts out from her bikini top. She is already getting tan lines, which makes her sexy in a whole new way. He rolls her over and gets on top, but his pulse throbs straight up his neck into his swollen nose. He falls back down onto the sheets.

"You better stay on top. My head might explode."

"No complaining," Maggie giggles. "You promised."

They have nothing to do except to obliterate their distinctness from one another. He feels his pulse throb equally in his groin and his nose, but it matches the pulse he feels inside of her, until all pleasure and pain merge and they disappear into one wonderful ache with no end. And then the ache is released, and he feels the last six months end too, and he is free. Their vacation begins, and all memory of the TV show disappears.

They lie on the beach and fall asleep under palm trees while reading Elmore Leonard novels. They eat grilled fish burgers at a beachside cafe and gulp sweet rum drinks decorated with fruit slices and paper umbrellas. They get up early and order room service and watch the sun rise from their hotel window while eating sourdough toast slathered with jam and sipping Kona coffee. They swim in the clear ocean water and feel schools of small silver fish dart between their legs. They get massages in the hotel health spa, and use their hotel coupons to get discount tickets to the hotel luau. They watch beautiful Hawaiian girls do the hula in the warm ocean breeze, and see a dance performance that depicts the ancient sea voyages of the original Hawaiians – brave men and women of the South Pacific who followed the flight paths of migrating birds north until they discovered the most remote islands on earth. They walk on the beach at night, under so many stars, they can't pick out any constellations in the mass confusion.

The beaches and pools and restaurants are packed with tourists from every state in the U.S., from Japan, the Philippines, Korea, Latin America, and Germany. But Maggie and Paul speak to no one else and feel as if the island is theirs alone.

When his nose shrinks down to two times its normal size, Paul risks putting on a diving mask and sticks a snorkel in his mouth. His pain level triples, but he flashes Maggie the thumbs-up nonetheless, and her happy smile makes the pain worthwhile. They hang onto hotel boogie boards and kick out to the outcropping of black lava rock on one end of the beach and stare at tropical fish from a psychedelic dream.

They crawl into bed and make love at the end of every afternoon and watch how their skin turns a darker brown each day, set against the white sheets. After a long nap, they wake up and dress for dinner. Before going downstairs, Maggie gently pulls off the surgical tape from Paul's face, revealing a perfect white tan line across the bridge of his swollen nose, then applies a fresh strip to start the evening.

At the end of the first week, they've gone no further than five hundred yards from the hotel. They are in bliss. That night at dinner while they gaze out at the waves, a Japanese bride and groom walk by on the beach followed by a photographer who snaps the couple's wedding photos against a golden sunset framed by perfect palm trees. Maggie sighs as she watches them.

Paul smiles at her and winks. She blushes. At this moment, the idea of marriage doesn't seem so terrifying. Granted, he is on vacation and is only briefly in control of his life, which will change once he gets back to Los Angeles, where no job and new bills are waiting. But then again, what are his life choices? He can:

1) Dump Maggie and have wild casual sex with dozens of gorgeous women. This is the silly goal of every single man in Los Angeles, many of whom are better looking and better off than Paul. Plus, wild casual sex is never the goal for any woman. This choice is impossible unless you're a movie star.

2) Date Maggie forever. When he was twenty-one, dating someone for more than eight months WAS forever. Now six months pass every time he exhales, and Maggie will dump him a long time before "forever" ever rolls around.

3) Examine Reality. He's been avoiding this for years, but now is the time to face the truth. For years, he's been banking on his youth, talent, and potential, but now he is thirty-one and that mojo is running out. Talented twenty-somethings with amazing student films move to Los Angeles every day, ready to take his place. The odds of him making it huge are slim and getting slimmer, and he's losing time to have a more typical life. People settle into a marriage and a career by this age, and if he keeps hanging on for a bid at fame and fortune, he may lose his chance for a regular life and career.

He does have a good personality and is decent looking, but he's not getting any younger, and he's aged two years in the last six months. He can't do better than Maggie, but she sure can do better than him.

Like Rupert, that pompous tanned Englishman with the cultivated accent. Paul remembers what Sarah said in the laundry room. Maggie and that tea bag must have spent some time together, otherwise Sarah wouldn't have said anything. Paul shakes his head. This is torture, he can't think this way.

The photographer finishes and bows to the Japanese couple, and they bow back. Maggie stares as the groom leads his bride back up the beach, steadying her in the soft sand as she holds up the train of her wedding dress.

Paul touches Maggie's hand and squeezes. Maggie looks at him.

"What are you thinking about?" he asks.

"Nothing," she lies. "What are you thinking about?"

"How happy I am with you. And how I should try harder to make you happy."

She smiles and wipes away a tear. He hadn't mentioned marriage, but Paul sees it is enough for her to read a lifetime into it.

"What do you see in me, anyway?" Paul asks.

"I wonder that myself all the time," she says and laughs.

"Ouch," Paul says.

Maggie face turns serious. "You're talented. You work hard. You have integrity. You are kind and loving when you're not self-absorbed, and we have fun together…"

Maggie pauses.

"And?

"And I'm in love with you," she shrugs. "Sorry, I just am."

They stare at each other. This is beyond a movie moment. It's so real and genuine he wants to rip open his mental movie file cabinet and destroy every entry in it as fake and self-indulgent.

He holds both of her hands. "I love you, too. And I'm not sorry about it."

"Good. What are we going to do about it?" she asks.

Paul remembers something his grandfather said to him years ago, which only makes sense to him now:

When a man loves a woman, he never wants anything to change. When a woman loves a man, she sees all the possibilities and starts to plan.

"I need a new plan for my life," Paul says. "For our life."

Maggie closes her eyes and nods, as if Paul finally understands something she's known for a very long time.

CHAPTER 29

P aul and Maggie eat breakfast in their hotel room and plan what to do with the last three days of their vacation – take a boat to some other island? Explore a dormant volcano? Visit a flower farm? – when the room phone rings. They look at one another with fear and confusion. The phone hasn't made a noise in eleven days, why is it ringing now?

"Don't answer it," Maggie says.

But the phone doesn't stop ringing. Paul picks up. "Hello?"

"Damn, you're a hard man to find. Have you heard the news?"

It takes Paul a second to place the voice. "I'm on vacation, Joel."

Maggie hears the name, rolls her eyes and falls back onto the bed, and covers her face with both arms.

""The *Tribe* is a hit," Joel says.

"The Tribe?" Paul asks. "What's that?"

"That's what we renamed the movie. Not only did the kiddies win their time slot, they pulled in a twenty-share. We were in the top ten for the week."

That's not what Paul wanted to hear. The show was supposed to air and be forgotten by the time he got back to Los Angeles.

"Those promo guys did an amazing job. They ran twenty-second promo spots twice a night for the full week prior. By the time Tuesday night rolled around, even I was dying to see it."

"Congratulations." He covers the phone. "Maggie, the show was a hit."

"I figured," she says, still lying on the bed.

Paul turns back to the phone. "What was Dwight's reaction?"

"He saw the promos and went ballistic. I told him about your version – "

"You told him? Why?" Paul yells so loud his nose hurts for the first time in days.

"He's no idiot, Paul. He knew right away that it was you. Relax, he blames me. He knows you were just following your producer's orders, which I told him that he should have just done in the first place, instead of ignoring me. That's when he demanded to have his name removed from all the credits and he threatened to kill me."

"He threatened to kill you?"

"I don't care, they're moving me to an office on the studio lot and he can't get past security anyway. What should make him furious is how well the show did and his name isn't even on it. I'm more concerned about his agent, who keeps calling me. He'll be the head of CAA one day, so I can't afford to piss him off."

"Whose name is on it?" Paul winces, scared to hear what is coming next.

"Yours, of course."

Paul takes the phone from his ear and hits himself in the forehead with it, which he instantly regrets. He hears Joel yelling his name through the receiver.

Paul puts the receiver back to his ear. "I told you I only wanted an audio credit. You should have asked me first, Joel."

"The network insisted. I tried reaching you, but you were nowhere to be found. I had to drive by your place and find out from your neighbor, some tall Brit with a tan. He told me right away that you were thinking about Kauai and switched it to Kaanapali on Maui. Even gave me the name of the hotel."

Hearing that Rupert knew about his holiday vacation darkens his mood. Maggie sees the sour look on his face and shoots him a confused "what?" shrug.

"How soon can you get back here? Joel asks.

"I'm on vacation, I'm not coming back until Sunday."

Maggie sits up and wags her finger at him, warning him to proceed with caution.

"No good. Jedidiah Kincaid wants to meet with us Friday."

"Jedidiah Kincaid, the head of the network, wants to meet with us Friday," Paul repeats out loud to Maggie. She grabs a pillow, covers her face and screams into it. Paul motions for her to keep quiet. She twists the sheets and pounds the mattress in a silent mock seizure of frustration, then pops up and points her finger in his face. "Don't you dare end our vacation early. We earned this time together."

"He wants to meet with us? What for?" Paul asks.

"He wants to expand *The Tribe* into a series to air in the new year."

"A series?" Paul asks. "What are you talking about?"

"I'm talking about thirteen hours of prime-time television that you will be directing, and I'll be producing," Joel says.

"How is that possible? The tribe doesn't even exist anymore."

"So? We'll bring them back together again."

"And we'll do what? Shoot them while they pretend to be homeless? What kind of documentary is that?"

"This show stopped being a documentary a long time ago," Joel says. "So how soon can you get back here?"

Maggie sits on the edge of the bed and stares up at him with anxious fear, as if Paul were standing on the ledge of a skyscraper, ready to jump. Paul hangs up the phone. Maggie smiles with relief. The phone starts ringing again. Maggie reaches behind the end table and unplugs it from the wall.

"We have to change hotels," Paul says.

"No, we don't. Just ignore him."

"But what are we going to do?"

"Today we're visiting a dormant volcano. The bus leaves in twenty minutes."

Maggie showers and dresses while Paul hurries to the lobby store and buys film, magazines, some Japanese snacks, and bottled drinks.

Back in the room, Maggie blow dries her hair while Paul throws the purchases in a satchel.

"Pack a sweater. That volcano is high," Maggie yells over the noise of the hair dryer. "It's supposed to be cold up there."

Paul throws two sweaters into the satchel and they run out of their hotel room. They dash through the lobby and grab their bus tickets from the excursion desk. The concierge sees them as they run past the front desk and yells. "Mr. Franti! You have an urgent message!" Paul and Maggie escape out the front doors and onto the tour bus just before the doors close.

They put on their dark glasses and sink low into their seats as the bus pulls away.

"Don't worry," Maggie says. "We're on an island in the middle of the Pacific Ocean. He'll never find us."

She kisses him, and they hold hands and gaze out the window at the lush green hillsides, the bright blue ocean, and the fields of sugar cane streaking by. But Paul is not reassured. For the rest of day, he imagines the lengths to which Joel will go to reach him. Hours later, as they stare down into a volcano crater the size of Manhattan, Paul wants to crawl inside one of its cinder cones and hide. He wants to hide because he feels a tug of interest, and Joel knows it, and Joel will probably get on a plane to find him, so he can tug harder.

What good could ever come out of a crazy idea like this? There is no way it could ever work. Can't anybody see that? Yet Jedidiah Kincaid himself wants to meet him.

Jedidiah Kincaid, the mad TV prophet, is the grandson of Welsh coal miners and the son of a self-made man who made his first million pounds selling advertising on bus benches and in London Tube stations. Jedidiah took his father's business and transformed it into a billion-dollar company that owns newspapers, TV stations, a film studio, and a TV network. He should at least go and meet the man, Paul thinks.

He keeps his mouth shut, but Maggie senses that the walls of their castle of bliss have been breached. He is with her inside the volcano, but his thoughts are elsewhere.

The bus stops at a tropical flower farm on the way back down the volcano. Maggie and Paul and two dozen other tourists wander past strange flowers, until Maggie pulls Paul aside.

"You're not leaving. You earned this vacation, remember that."

Paul calms down. He remembers that Joel, and every boss he has ever had, could always make him feel like he owed them something, which is why Paul always agrees to every crazy task he gets handed. Paul knows he can say "no" to all of this. In fact, it's crucial that he learn to say "no," because if they can sucker him into saying "yes," he'll never get what he wants.

When they get back to their hotel room there is a pile of urgent call messages that the hotel staff slid under the door. Maggie tosses them all away, then they both stare at the phone, still expecting it to ring even though it's not even plugged in.

"We'll be fine. Jedidiah Kincaid and Joel Cuvney both take vacations, and so can you," she says, and stroking his arm. "Let's change your nose bandage."

"Should I do it?"

Maggie doesn't answer. She cuts off a new strip of surgical tape, lifts off the old piece and lays the new tape across the bridge of his nose. "You're healing, I think."

"You didn't answer my question."

"I can't answer that for you. It's your life."

"I think I need an agent."

Maggie sighs. "If you want, I can ask the Screaming Asshole for advice. Crushing network producers like Joel is one of his favorite hobbies."

Maggie stares at him with a blank face, the kind of empty look that he can use in an edit bay, because it can mean anything – anger, hunger, disdain, fear – but not love. He is not feeling love emanating from her right now.

If he pursues this, his life will change.

He'd be riding a rollercoaster, alongside Jedidiah Kincaid and Joel Cuvney, with Trent, Jodi, Ilima, and Duncan (if he could ever find him again). The Screaming Asshole will probably want to jump on board and get a piece of it, while Dwight would try to destroy it completely. Not a fun ride.

What could he gain? Financial freedom, maybe. No more worries about repo men, broken noses, which bills to pay first, or whether he can afford a car or a vacation. He could hire people to help him finish his film, instead of doing every job himself.

What could he lose? Time. His life wouldn't be his own. He wouldn't take another vacation anytime soon. He might not even have time for Maggie, and he didn't want to lose her.

One thing is certain, however; this show will happen, with or without him. The network feels like it has a hit on its hands, and if he turns it down, they'll find someone else to do it, within a day. This is the Hollywood brass ring, and it's right in front of him. It's not the ring he's dreamed of grabbing – it's not a prestigious movie or TV drama, but it is still a brass ring, and one that he created. He is the one who found a story within the hours of footage, and connected with Duncan and saw that he could be a star. He'd be a fool to walk away and let someone else take it.

He wants both. With Maggie, he has a warm, loving, solid partner – a life partner. This could be their first success together as a power couple. Duncan is "watchable," with endless charisma. If Paul can find a way to harness that charisma, he could turn Duncan into a movie star. Hell, he could run for public office.

He must try to do it. When you get an invitation to the casino, you play. But the idea terrifies and nauseates him. He clutches his gut.

Maggie stands up from the corner of the bed and holds Paul's hands in hers. "How do you feel right now?" Maggie asks. "Deep down inside?"

"Sick to my stomach."

"Like you did the entire time you were working on the show before?"

"Except worse."

"What makes you think it will be any different this time?"

Paul stares at Maggie. She isn't pushing him one way or the other. She's trying to get him to feel and know and be sure of what he really wants, instead of being impulsive and reactive and just picking the path that's in front of him.

"Like leads to like," Paul says.

Maggie nods and lets go of his hands. "Right. Like leads to like."

It's true in any career. Accounting leads to accounting, law leads to more law, medicine leads to medicine, comedy leads to comedy, and crazy unhinged fake reality shows lead to more unhinged fake reality shows. This could be his life.

Paul glances over his shoulder and sees the beautiful sun sinking behind the island of Lanai. He has had more fun and more real moments in the past two weeks than he has had since coming to Los Angeles, and he hasn't watched TV or movies or thought about his own film the entire time. He feels alive – or, he did until the phone rang this morning.

He has his answer. It's "no." It's time to crawl out of the cave and blink at the sun and choose real life instead of movies and TV and this insane plate-spinning drama, that gets whipped up into a frenzy for no good reason.

There are a hundred careers for him, not just this one, and Maggie believes in him. Opportunity will knock again. He doesn't know what that is yet, but it will make him feel open and happy and challenged and ready to take on the world, like he does when he's with Maggie. Like he feels right now.

"I'm not doing it. If I did, I think it would drive me insane."

Maggie smiles, and wipes away a tear. "I agree."

"I won't have a job. I don't know how I'll pay my share of the rent."

"We'll figure that out. It's better for you to be sane, I think." She laughs and sniffles and wipes more tears away.

They face each other in the middle of the hotel room, laughing, almost awkward with each other, living a moment they will both remember forever as the moment when they decided. When their real life began.

"Let's eat dinner."

"Let me blow my nose and wash my face," Maggie says. She pecks him on the lips and goes into the bathroom.

Paul walks out onto the balcony and stares at the setting sun. He feels something he's never felt before. He feels part of the world for once, instead of outside watching it, and it feels nice.

He looks down at the people walking along the meandering garden path that runs between the different hotels. One man stands in the middle of the path, blocking people until he can make them look at a photograph in his hand. They all shake their heads "no" and push past him.

The man is dressed in jeans and a pullover shirt, more appropriate to Los Angeles than Hawaii. His body language seems familiar, but he can't place it…

The man glances up and sees him on the balcony. It's Dwight.

The sick feeling returns. Paul wants to step back, but he's frozen. Dwight points at him, and makes a motion with his thumb like he's firing a gun.

The End of Book 1

Find more writing and free downloads at: IanBullAuthor.com

Or just email me and I'll send you something for free:

IanBullAuthor@gmail.com

Please write a review of this book. It would be a big help.

Special Thanks to:
My wife, Robin Berlin, and my daughter, Lily Faith Berlin Bull.

Made in United States
Troutdale, OR
08/11/2024

21896396R10137